More Praise For
James S. Gardner's
Dark Continent Chronicles

"I highly recommend The Lion Killer. I have seldom come across such fine descriptive writing in a thriller."

—James Patterson

America's Best-Selling author

———————

"A riveting thriller with twists and turns galore."

—Robert Halmi Jr

Emmy and Golden Globe Award winning Executive Producer of "Lonesome Dove"

———————

"Few really good books come out of Africa, but James Gardner's 'The Lion Killer' is one of those few. It's easy to see that Gardner has been there and that he understood what he saw. His powerful writing illuminates the Dark Continent."

—Nelson DeMille

New York Times Best-Selling author

"Sara and I were blown out of our chairs by the power of your presentation and we wish you a whole lot of luck with 'The Lion Killer'!"

—Barry Farber

National talk radio host

"'The Lion Killer' is an extraordinary read on an extraordinary mission. For those that actually consider the future of Africa, it may very well change their perspective."

—Douglas Harrington

Hamptons.com

"Gardner's story telling approach follows in the path of Dashiell Hammett. "Life is disposable; the Land is beautiful and the search is fatal."

—James Edstrom

Times Square Gossip

"In this book, James Gardner takes you on a thrill-ride through so many terrifying places and events in darkest Africa, you have to pull the covers over your head to finish it.

Hell of a trip for us adventure readers!"

—Dan Jenkins, Novelist & Journalist

THE LAST RHINO

THE DARK CONTINENT SERIES BOOK IV

JAMES GARDNER

PENNINGTON PUBLISHERS

PENNINGTON PUBLISHERS

ISBN: 978-1-935827-2-76
Trade Paperback
© Copyright 2016 James Gardner
All Rights Reserved

Requests for information should be addressed to:
Pennington Publishers, Inc.
PO Box 718
Decatur, GA 30031

Pennington Publishers and the Pennington logo
are imprints of Pennington Publishers, Inc.

Cover design: Donald Brennan / YakRider Media
Interior design: Donald Brennan / YakRider Media

Artwork and illustrations by Larry Norton and used by
permission.

Printed in the U.S.A.

For the game rangers who risk their lives
protecting Africa's endangered animals

ACKNOWLEDGEMENTS

I would like to thank my editors, Lynn Denney, Barbara Gardner, R.C. Knutsen and editor/publisher, Donald Brennan.

I am especially grateful for the illustrations by one of Africa's most gifted artists, Larry Norton.

—JG

The publisher also would like to express gratitude to Larry Norton for permission to use his exceptional and compelling art of Africa.

—DB

About the Author

James Gardner's first African safari was in 1968. Subsequently, he's made twenty-five trips to Africa. He has written numerous magazine and newspaper articles about modern Africa, its culture, its people, and the difficulties they face. He is author of *The Dark Continent Chronicles*, a series of political thrillers that includes *The Lion Killer*, *The Zambezi Vendetta*, *The Honeyguide* and *The Last Rhino*.

He is also an award-winning screenplay writer, winning at the Slamdance and L.A. Screenwriter's competitions.

He is an avid animal wildlife conservationist.

James was interviewed on PBS at WXEL's arts talk show *Between the Covers*, hosted by Ann Bocock.

About the Artist

Born in Zimbabwe in 1963, Larry Norton grew up on a game farm in north-east Zimbabwe. He started drawing as a boy and in 1988 began a professional career. Since then he has exhibited around the world including several successful exhibitions in New York and London.

He works in oils, water colour, charcoal and pencil and specializes in African subjects, including wildlife, landscape and people of the continent.

www.larrynorton.co.za
E-mail:- info@larrynorton.co.za
P.O. Box CT 534
Victoria Falls, Zimbabwe

JAMES GARDNER

Prologue
Victoria Falls, Zimbabwe
Stanley's Bar in the Victoria Falls Hotel

Gentlemen, name your poison?" The African bartender wore a red fez with a black tassel dangling to one side.

"Two Dewar's straight up." Rigby Croxford, the protagonist, tossed the first half of the unedited novel, The Last Rhino, on the bar. "You nailed it."

The author, James Gardner, patted the dogeared manuscript. "What about accuracy?"

After a prolonged sip, Croxford said, "This is exactly what happened up until Penny died. It was spot-on. I scribbled suggestions on the margins, like you asked me. Nothing earthshaking, mind you. Use or ignore them. It's your call."

Gardner eyed Croxford's handwritten notes. "Is that for me?"

"Indeed. It describes everything that happened after I left Dar es Salaam." Croxford stared sightlessly at the mist rising above Victoria Falls. "Brought back some bloody unpleasant memories, but it's done."

After draining the last drop of Scotch, Gardner placed his glass on the bar. He picked up Croxford's notes. "I look forward to reading this. It'll take me six months to do my thing. After that, there's the editing. He hesitated and then added, "Will the book put you at risk? I mean with the government."

"Perhaps, but it's a risk worth taking."

"I can omit anything that might make trouble for you. Just say the word."

Croxford said, "An old Swahili proverb says, 'A lie has many variations, but the truth only one.'"

"And I think Mahatma Gandhi wrote, 'Truth never damages a just cause,'" Gardner said.

"If memory serves, they killed Gandhi," Croxford mentioned.

Gardner sighed and nodded.

1

Confucius: Before you embark on a journey of revenge,
dig two graves.

The funeral procession trudged slowly up the hill to Helen
Croxford's grave. The younger mourners assisted the
elderly. What had been weedy and unattended was now planted
in orange flame lilies. One hundred years of wind and rain had
etched the older headstones. The newer grave markers bore the
names of black Africans. During her life, Helen had insisted on an
inclusive graveyard. She was a lone voice for the voiceless. Helen's
final resting place was nestled between two leafless Rhodesian
teak trees. The tree's arthritic limbs beckoned the faithful.

The freshly-turned grave dirt smelled musty. The wind
quickened. An angry sky embedded with churning purple clouds
obscured the sun. Ragged snakes of white lightning and low
rumbling promised rain. And then, as if ordered by a higher power,
the sky cleared allowing brilliant rays of sunlight to illuminate
Helen's grave. The sobbing was amplified. Bereaved women wept.
Men consoled the anguished. Mourners crossed themselves and
looked skyward. Children huddled between their parents.

Dr. Helen Croxford had always wanted an African funeral. A
Shona burial calls for a black iron pot to be placed next to the
gravesite. Wooden sticks were handed to the attendees as they
filed past the receiving line that included Helen's husband, Rigby
Croxford, their daughter and her grandson.

If the departed treated the person fairly, a stick was to be dropped into the pot. If the deceased had wronged the person, a stick would be retrieved. The length and magnitude of the eulogies were linked to the number of sticks in the funeral pot. Helen's pot was brimming. The black minister was long-winded. The tortuous service seemed never-ending.

The singing died down gradually and stopped. A blood-curdling scream had interrupted the hymn, "Abide with Me." All eyes were drawn to a rail-thin woman rolling on the ground. Her arms and legs flailed about like they were boneless. As she chanted, white foam collected in the corners of her mouth. Her eyes had a wild deranged look. The crowd began to clap in rhythm with her bizarre incantation. Abruptly, her trance ended. The dazed woman appeared totally oblivious. The crowd resumed their hymn singing as if nothing had happened.

For obvious reasons, African burials are hasty affairs. Dr. Helen Croxford was killed on a moonless night. She was laid to rest the following afternoon on a hilltop overlooking the medical clinic that had been her life's work. On the night she died, her husband was leading an anti-poaching patrol in southern Zimbabwe. It took four days for the news of his wife's death to reach Rigby Croxford. The Criminal Investigation Department concluded that the cause of her death was "accidental."

The official report stated:

Dr. Helen Croxford and a nurse, Mary Abeko, were traveling at a high rate of speed on unlit foggy roads. After rounding a sharp bend, their vehicle struck a donkey cart. Both occupants were fatally injured as was the man driving the cart. According to sources, Dr. Croxford was making an emergency medical call.

The last line read, "The husband, Mister Rigby Croxford, and the deceased woman's daughter, Dr. Christine Croxford, have been notified. This case is closed."

Rigby didn't challenge the CID's postmortem inquiry, but he suspected foul play. There were too many unanswered questions. Why was a donkey cart loaded with rocks traveling at night? Why didn't the person seeking his wife's medical help come forward? What happened to the donkey-cart driver's body? And there was his wife's ongoing campaign against the government's finance minister, Dkari Sibanda, for his alleged complicity in the illegal wildlife trade.

Helen's memorial was held one month after her interment. Her patients were generally poor. Sometimes she bartered medical services for chickens or goats. Many times, her treatments were given *pro-bono*. She delivered babies in darkened huts. She saved many lives. Accordingly, her memorial was well-attended. Raggedly dressed Africans arrived in overstuffed buses and flatbed trucks. Some attendees walked many miles to get there. The country's president and his political entourage, accompanied by bodyguards, arrived in black Mercedes Benzes. They wore expensive Italian suits and ill-fitting English shoes.

The crowd acknowledged the dignitaries with weak compulsory applause.

A spokesman for the president, a sinister weasel of a man with the bulging red eyes of a dope smoker, approached the Croxfords. He spoke softly. "His Excellency wishes to express his sympathy."

Rigby was incensed. "You can tell that..."

Rigby's daughter interrupted her father. "Tell the president we value his kindness." She glared at her father. The spokesman scurried back to the president. After conferring with his spokesman the president smiled. Behind his horn-rimmed glasses hid the predatory eyes of a spitting cobra. Rigby was even more enraged.

Christine frowned. "No sense making him an enemy."

Rigby said, "Enemy? You don't get it. He hates us. I'll see him in hell."

To say most Africans are superstitious is not overstated. Even the educated believe the departed can wreak havoc on the living. Rigby knew that the person responsible for Helen Croxford's death would never attend his wife's memorial service. Rigby scanned the crowd. Using a Bible as a screen, he whispered to his friend, Jedediah, "So, Sibanda's a no-show. I told you it was him. Killing that bastard will be my pleasure." Rigby's words were more for himself

Jed glanced over both shoulders. Dropping his voice to a conspiratorial level, he said, "It won't be easy. Not with his bodyguards."

"Bodyguards, my ass. Trust me. As God is my witness, his days are limited."

Rigby's daughter leaned in. What she heard made her blanch. "This isn't the proper time or place to be talking about killing."

"What do you think I did in the war?"

"The war is finished."

"Not for me it isn't. 'Vengeance is mine, sayeth the Lord,'"

"You're not God."

"Lucky for Mister Sibanda, I'm *not*. Let's just say, I aim to do His work."

The thunderstorm had grown to biblical proportions. After expressing their gratitude to the mourners, the Croxfords walked single file down the hill, disappearing into the downpour.

James Gardner

2

Rigby Croxford was up before sunrise. His geriatric Land Rover was loaded with enough supplies for two weeks in the bush. Jedediah and two Matabele trackers stood next to the vehicle smoking their first cigarettes of the day. Rigby's daughter made a last-minute appeal, but her opposition to her father's anti-poaching patrols fell on deaf ears. Deep down, she knew he needed the diversion. It was a tearful goodbye. He tossed her a wink, gave her thumbs-up and drove away. Christine stood on the veranda watching his taillights fade into the predawn darkness.

It's a ten-hour drive to the Chizarira Game Reserve. Under normal circumstances, he would stop and visit friends along the way to break up the monotony, but he couldn't stomach hearing more condolences. His only stop was at an anti-poaching encampment near the entrance to the Hwange National Game Park. The head ranger was a lanky Matabele with an infectious smile and perfect teeth.

After they exchanged greetings, the ranger recanted the local gossip. One of Hwange's male lions had been baited into an adjoining hunting preserve. The lion, nicknamed Cecil, had been killed by an American bow hunter. A new male lion had already taken over the pride. Instinctually, the male had killed the cubs thereby ensuring his legacy.

The ranger said that so many male lions were being killed by hunters and poachers, most prides were on the verge of collapse.

As they parted company, the ranger warned, "*Usale kuhle*. Go well, my friend. Please be watchful. We have reports of poachers operating in your area."

Rigby said, "Keep up the good work. See you soon."

The ranger waved goodbye.

The Chizarira Game Reserve lies on the edge of the Great Zambezi Escarpment. The game park is home to Zimbabwe's dwindling rhino population. The mountainous reserve contains many deep gorges and steep hillsides spotted by mountain acacias and occasional baobab trees.

They pitched their tents on a sand bluff overlooking an oxbow in the Busi River. The river would become a raging torrent during the rainy season, but now the sandy riverbed was strewn with elephant-dung heaps and animal trails.

At dusk, Rigby and Jed watched some elephants drinking from an excavated borehole in the river. Baby elephants sought protection between their mothers' legs. Two adolescents locked trunks in a good-natured tug-of-war. When their game became too rowdy, the herd's matriarch separated them. A squealing female tried to suckle her mother, but the pregnant cow gently pushed her away. An old bull ranging on the herd's periphery raised his trunk tasting the air for receptive females.

His thick black lashes hampered his vision, but something had unnerved him. He rumbled a low warning. The herd moved slowly away and disappeared into a stand of mopani trees. Over the next few days, Rigby's anti-poaching patrols ventured deeper into the game reserve. They destroyed hundreds of wire snares used by poachers to entrap animals.

Life is hard in Africa. Rigby gave the subsistence poachers a pass, but not the ivory and rhino poachers. Their greed was destroying Zimbabwe's heritage. For these endangered animal exterminators, he gave no quarter.

On the fifth day, they split up into two patrols. Rigby and Jed followed the riverbed south. The two Matabele trackers set off in the opposite direction. The river's soft sand and mud-cracks slowed down their progress. The hours passed slowly. Rigby's rifle seemed to grow heavier as the sun sapped his enthusiasm. He shifted his weapon from one shoulder to the other. The silence gave him time to think about his wife. The thoughts made him feel so weak-kneed, he kept stumbling. He cleared his mind and concentrated on the moment.

Jed stopped dead in his tracks. He used his walking stick to point at human footprints in the sand.

Rigby observed, "So, that's why we're not seeing fresh elephant spoor. Poachers spooked them."

They quickened their pace. The poachers had covered their tracks, but not enough to fool Jed. He used shortcuts avoiding the heaviest thorn thickets.

As the trail got hotter he quickened the pace. After three hours of hard slugging, Rigby said, "Let's rest before you die from a heart attack."

Jed hadn't broken a sweat. "Must I carry you on my back?"

Rigby quipped, "A bull elephant takes his time, but he always covers the most females." His retort made Jed smile.

Rigby smoked a cigarette under a teak tree while Jed climbed a sandstone kopje. This time Rigby daydreamed about killing the man responsible for his wife's death. He felt reinvigorated.

Jed used the alarm-call of a hornbill to get Rigby's attention. He pointed at a spiral of circling vultures on the horizon.

Both men started to run. As they got closer to the vultures, Rigby grew more cautious. He forced Jed to slowdown to a trot and finally to a walk. An unusual hush set in. Even the cooing doves were silenced. It was quiet enough to hear Jed's stomach growl. The shrill yelps of a black-backed jackal gave them pause. They stood motionless for a few long minutes. The jackal emerged from the underbrush. Jed pointed at something only he could see. Rigby followed him into a hook-thorn thicket. It was a de-horned rhino carcass someone had covered with tree branches. The female's prolapsed uterus was teeming with squirming white maggots. Blowflies thickened the air.

Jed knelt in the sand examining a misshapen footprint. "I know this one—a crippled Bushman. He is known as *Kgosi*."

"How old is his spoor?" Rigby asked covering his nose and mouth with a red-checkered bandana.

Jed reached down, scooped up a fistful of sand and let the dirt sift though his fingers. "He was here yesterday just before nightfall."

Rigby thought he saw the rhino's eyelash twitch. He got down on all fours and placed his face against her nostrils. "Christ, she's still breathing." Without hesitating he stuck the muzzle of his rifle into her ear and pulled the trigger. The animal's legs stiffened. She bellowed and lay still. The last convulsive seizure ejected a stillborn calf.

Rigby squashed a cigarette butt with his heel. He chambered another round into his .458 Winchester and swung it up onto his shoulder. "He can't get far."

Jed moved over the sand like a ballet dancer, but Rigby's bulk made the footslogging   difficult. After two more hours of hard marching, Jed stopped. The stench of death had carried on the wind. Rigby pointed at a rocky outcropping, which they climbed.

With the sun fading behind them, they peeked over the rim. What they saw was hellish. Massacred elephants lay everywhere. Rigby handed his binoculars to Jed. The graying sky was filled with carrion eaters. A shirtless African barked orders. Men chopped out tusks with hand-axes. Other men stacked the ivory in graded piles. Two men tended meat on a smoking fire. They heard death bellowing. A poacher hacked off the tusks of a dying elephant too sick to resist.

Rigby whispered, "I've seen enough." He pulled Jed back from the rim. After sliding down the hill, they ran until they were out of earshot. Rigby retrieved his sat phone and called the ranger station. He gave the GPS coordinates and asked for backup. The radio operator said that driving at night was too dangerous. Park rangers would arrive on sight at first light.

Rigby and Jed settled in for a cold, sleepless night.

The mournful cooing of ringed-neck doves promised an artist's-easel sunrise, but there was no sign of it yet. The eastern sky was clearing, but the horizon was still hazy. The first sunrays revealed night dew glistening on diamond-shaped spider webs attached to the bulrushes surrounding a cocoa-colored waterhole. Roasting white-backed vultures and marabou storks bore witness to a massacre. Dead elephants congested the waterhole, their wrinkled carcasses speckled by white bird feces. The more scavenged ones resembled giant deflated gray balloons.

All were left faceless. Spotted hyenas and jackals, having

gorged on the cyanide-laced elephant meat, lay dead or too sick to move. Early rains would tease the land but not enough to dilute the poison. The deathtrap would continue killing until the rains came.

Rigby and Jed reassured each other. The rangers would be arriving any minute. Rigby kept glancing at his wristwatch. Doubts began to form.

They heard the distant beat of a helicopter. Within seconds, a Bell-Jet Ranger was   hovering over the waterhole.

The rotor-wash created a swirling orange dust cloud. The noise frightened the vultures. Heavy bellies lengthened their lumbering hop-skipping takeoffs. Slowly they gained altitude and rejoined the circling holding pattern above the massacre.

Dkari Sibanda and his son, Michael, ducked underneath the spinning rotors. They were met by the leader of the poaching gang. They inspected the ivory piles. Some of the tusks were no longer than a man's forearm. There were kudu, zebra and impala skins and tangles of antlers laid out. They examined elephant hair used for bracelets and severed feet that would be fashioned into footstools. One poacher pulled back a tarpaulin revealing lion organs and bones. Sibanda picked up a bone and spoke to his son. "Asians believe this is medicine. And they call us ignorant savages." Sibanda cupped his hand to conceal his voice. "Pay them before the Chinaman arrives. If he finds out how little money we give them, he'll haggle us to death. You must learn these things well, my son. From this day forward, you will be in charge."

Sibanda's son paid each man separately. As they received their money, they clapped their hands in a traditional show of gratitude. The last man in the queue was ancient. He was a clubfooted Bushman. His yellowish belly skin sagged in folded layers.

His winkled cadaverous face featured eyes clouded by cataracts. He wore a woolen ski cap and unlaced sneakers. The old man grabbed Sibanda's son's hand and whispered proudly in broken English, "I have something very special for your father."

Sibanda's son shouted, "Papa, this one wishes to speak to you."

After conversing, Dkari Sibanda followed the old man into the underbrush. Sibanda's newfound prosperity had provided him with all of the trappings of a wealthy African, including obesity. Even hampered by a clubfoot, the poacher had to stop and wait for him. The soft sand took a toll on Sibanda. He shrugged off his shirt. Rivers of sweat streaked his pendulous breasts before disappearing into an enormous waistline. He bent over gasping for air. "This better be good, old man."

The old Bushman reassured Sibanda. "What I have will please you."

Through clenched teeth Sibanda hissed, "For your sake, it better."

"What we seek is near." To Bushmen, the meaning of the word 'near' is ill-defined. They walked for the better part of an hour. Finally, they stopped at the base of a decaying baobab tree. Sibanda leaned against the tree trying to catch his breath. Hidden deep in the rotting trunk was something wrapped in a filthy gunnysack. The poacher grinned as Sibanda slowly unveiled a rhino's horn. Sibanda's eyes bugged out. He cradled the horn like a father holding his firstborn child. He tried to speak, but the exertion had robbed his wind. After clearing his throat, he croaked, "Old father, you've made me very happy." He reached into both pockets and grabbed fistfuls of Zimbabwe dollars. After second thoughts, he took off his gold wristwatch and handed it to the old man.

"You can trade the watch for a wife or goats. Bring me more

like this one and I'll make you richer than your wildest dreams." The old man's smile was toothless. He danced a jig in the sand admiring his new watch.

The walk back wasn't as difficult for Sibanda. Greed had renewed him. After they parted company, Sibanda stored the rhino horn in the baggage compartment of his Bell-Jet Ranger.

He made mental calculations. The horn could fetch at least two-hundred thousand in U.S. dollars. The ivory business was profitable, but paled by comparison to rhino horn. The ivory would bring around five hundred dollars per kilogram. At rock bottom, the lion organs and bones were worth another fifty thousand. The hides weren't worth enough to worry about. He owed the poachers maybe fifty thousand at best, give or take. And there were some bribes to pay, but overall this will have been a profitable day. Very profitable indeed, he mused.

Rigby and Jed watched from the vantage point of the hilltop. Jed scanned the horizon hoping to see road dust kicked up by the approaching ranger patrol. He saw nothing. Rigby put his rifle's crosshairs in the middle of Dkari Sibanda's forehead. As he mock-fired he whispered, "Ka-pow." Jed, who was holding his breath, exhaled.

His apprehension resurfaced. "The rangers aren't coming. Damn them to hell."

Jed added, "It's finished then."

"No fucking way," said Rigby. He scrambled down the back of the hill, ran a few hundred meters and redialed his sat phone. No one answered...

The poachers nicknamed him, Uncle Mao, because his Chinese name, Zhang Wei, was too slippery on their African tongues. He was a small rat-faced man. Overhanging teeth distorted his pigeon English. Between incomplete sentences, he cleared his throat, spat yellow phlegm on the ground and kicked sand over the blobs. Mao was never without his abacus, which he used to make almost instant computations.

Mao blinked away the annoying blowflies. "Africa only good for making money. Not good place to live. Some of this ivory too small. Cannot pay you so much this time. Carvers only want big ivory."

It was a game they'd played many times. Sibanda sighed dramatically. "The ivory is the same as the last time. Okay, how much for the lot?"

Mao's slammed the abacus beads back and forth. "Three hundred and fifty, the most I can pay you. You should take it."

It was a short time before Sibanda responded. He swatted unsuccessfully at a fly and shook his head. He was distracted by a baby elephant squealing for its dead mother's udder. "Will someone kill that thing? I can't think." Two poachers picked up their hand-axes and ran after the tiny elephant. The fear of humans renewed the baby elephant's survival instinct. Their pursuit ended when the elephant ducked into a thicket of wild rose bushes.

Without the protection of the herd, the motherless elephant would become a victim of the night.

Sibanda wagged his chubby finger in Mao's face and raised his voice, "You thief! You think I don't know the ivory market. Why, you'll get a thousand per kilo or maybe even more. You must think I'm a damn fool. You're not the only buyer, you know."

Mao knew Sibanda was bluffing. Mao wiped sweat from his brow and flicked it. Undeterred, he said, "I take big risk. Many... many greedy African people want bribes. You very hard bargainer. I go up four hundred and twenty-five, but not a penny more." His boney shoulders sagged in exaggerated defeat. "If you smart you take it."

Sibanda ignored him. "How about five hundred, and you've got yourself a deal."

Mao shook his head and spraying spittle between his front teeth countered at four-fifty.

"It's not enough," said Sibanda stepping just out of Mao's spitting range. "Let's say, four hundred seventy-five in U.S. dollars and call it a day. That's my final price. Take it or leave it."

They shook hands sealing the transaction. Mao unconsciously wiped his hand on his pants. "Now, let's talk about rhino horn."

"What horn?" Sibanda asked faking ignorance. I should have seen this coming, he thought.

"The rhino horn you hide in helicopter. I pay you big-big money."

Sibanda knew one of the poachers had tipped off Mao. "The horn is not for sale. Not today it isn't."

Mao coughed productively and spat as if to cleanse his mouth of a foul tasting substance. He sneezed violently. "Everything in Africa for sale—including the people."

Sibanda glared at him. The rhino horn would go unsold.

Mao stacked tightly wrapped bundles of currency on a truck's bonnet. Sibanda's son stuffed the money into two duffle bags.

Mao said, "You change mind about horn, let me know. I pay you top price in cash."

Sibanda sneered. "Let me think about it." He twirled his finger at the pilot indicating his desire to leave. Sibanda's son walked his father to the idling Jet Ranger.

Rigby whispered, "God damn it, he's getting away." He raised his weapon, but Jed prevented him from firing. "They are many and we are two."

"Go, before you get shot," Rigby ordered.

Jed shook his head vehemently. "I'm not running. If they kill you, they must kill me."

"You damn fool, suit yourself."

A quick smile curled the corners of Jed's mouth.

Sibanda yelled to his son over the helicopter's spoiling turbine. "Make sure all of this ivory gets weighed. Always be wary of the yellow man, my son. The white Rhodesians were wicked devils, but at least you could trust them. These Chinese feed like hyenas. They leave nothing, not even food for the worms." He hugged his son. "You've made me very proud today. Next week, we'll fly down to Cape Town. I have a gift for you."

"What did you buy me, papa?"

"A red Mercedes."

The helicopter's liftoff dusted the elephant carcasses. An orange plume trailed the first truck already underway to Mozambique. Its cargo would be offloaded into a freighter bound for Hong Kong. Sibanda patted the duffle bags on the seat next to him. He waved to his son as he flew overhead.

Rigby jumped up firing his weapon, but the helicopter was so far out of range the occupants didn't even know they were taking fire. It disappeared over the horizon. The hilltop exploded in a hail of gunfire. Bullets cracked and whistled, kicking up clumps of dirt and rocks. Rigby and Jed hunkered down, waiting for a lull. When the shots subsided, they scrambled down the back of the hill and disappeared into the underbrush.

The ceasefire was momentary. The poachers reloaded their AKs and commenced shooting blindly. Sibanda's son ran forward shouting to stop firing, but his voice succumbed to the sound of gunfire. He turned around and raised his arms. An errant AK round hit him just above the right eye-socket. The entry wound was tiny. The exit wound blew out the back of his skull.

The five-hour march back to the Busi River campsite was grueling. When Rigby and Jed finally arrived they were met by two park rangers and four CID policemen. The two Matabele trackers were handcuffed and lay face down in the dirt.

Rigby bellowed, "What's going on here?"

Rigby had had dealings with the policeman in charge before. He was a surly dark toad of a man with a shiny baldhead and half-mast eyes. He stepped forward, strutting like a peacock. "So it's Mr. Croxford, the man who values animals more than men."

Rigby ignored him and addressed the rangers. "What happened today? Where were you?" The rangers looked away guiltily. Disgusted, Jed expectorated in the dirt.

"Never mind them, Mr. Croxford. You've got a serious problem."

"You don't say. What kind of nonsense have you dreamed up this time?"

"I'm arresting you for the murder of Michael Sibanda."

Rigby's face registered shock. "Rubbish! I don't know what you're talking about."

"A magistrate will decide your fate. In the meantime, I'll have your weapon, sir."

Rigby handed the policeman his Winchester. "Take it. This government has taken everything from me. You might as well have the last thing I own."

The court ruled that Rigby Croxford and Jed were flight risks. The local magistrate ordered that the defendants be jailed in a maximum security prison pending their trial. They were driven straight to Hwange Prison.

Political incarcerations are not uncommon in Zimbabwe. Consequently, this wasn't Rigby's first time in prison. Jed's guilt was one by association. Not only was the charge extremely serious, a powerful politician was pulling the strings.

The first night in prison is always the hardest. The prison cellblock was designed for fifty prisoners, now it housed one hundred inmates. The night sounds were a cacophony of bronchial rattles, hacking coughs, wheezes and snoring.

The gag producing stench of unwashed bodies and excrement saturated the air.

There was another problem. Rigby was seen as a person of special interest by the corrupt government. Black zealots wanted to rid Zimbabwe of what they called the undesirable white elements in our society. His deportation had always been the government's aim. As a white farmer, he was the perfect scapegoat. When he lost his farm, the government assumed he would emigrate. They underestimated his resolve.

The president of Zimbabwe had been a noncombatant in the Rhodesian Bush War. The soldiers who did the actual fighting demanded to be compensated for military services rendered. The country's only real assets were the white-owned farms. After the first farm was taken, the confiscation snowballed. Zimbabwe's white population had been reduced from three hundred thousand to less than fifty thousand in only thirty years. Zimbabwe's racial cleansing wasn't unusual. It was happening all over Africa. White colonialists had been inept caretakers. This was retribution for their cruel treatment of black Africans.

The clock turned slowly for Rigby and Jed. Hours became tedious days and those long days turned into endless weeks. Their spirits, low enough to begin with, sank to new depths. Rations were withheld. Beatings were commonplace. They believed their exculpation was inevitable, but the deplorable conditions took a toll. Lesser men would have succumbed. They endured the unendurable. Time hung heavy.

3

Beira, Mozambique

Zhang Wei, also known as Uncle Mao, stood on the bridge next to the captain of the Chinese bulk carrier, Flying Dragon. Loading at the port in Beira made Wei edgy. Hidden beneath the Zambian copper mined and smelted into ingots were ten shipping receptacles containing five tons of African ivory destined for Shanghai, China. Also hidden deep in the bowels of the ship was one hundred kilograms of rhino horn. Twenty-five rhinos had been killed in western Mozambique bordering the Kruger National Park in South Africa. Four more had been poached in Zimbabwe.

Bribes were paid. Wei's Vietnamese liaison in Da Nang would pay additional bribes. The rhino horn cargo was scheduled to be unloaded for overland shipment to Hai Phong in the north.

Zhang Wei would not make the eight-thousand kilometer journey by sea. He preferred making the roundtrips to and from Shanghai in a chartered jet. Wei may have looked and dressed like a coolie, but he was a millionaire many times over. Not only was he skimming a few kilos of rhino horn from every shipment, he had been hoarding ivory for years. His long-term investment strategy was intuitive.

He reasoned that if elephants and rhinos edged closer to extinction the price for both horn and ivory would have to increase. In one decade the price of ivory had increased tenfold.

Rhino horn was now more valuable than gold. Poachers were killing 30,000 African elephants per year. The total African elephant population is only 400,000 animals. Rhinos were being decimated at an unsustainable rate. In just three years, 3,394 rhinos were killed in southern Africa. The entire rhino population stood at 25,000 animals.

The make-believe medicinal properties created an insatiable demand for rhino horn in Vietnam. Increased levels of disposable income skewed the supply versus demand equation. The rhino population was being decimated. Wei believed the extinction of both endangered species would drive prices to stratospheric levels.

Beijing's leaders had been wringing their hands in public about ending the illicit wildlife trade, but behind the scenes they were actively encouraging the ivory trade by licensing factories and retail outlets specializing in carved ivory products. The government declared that ivory carving was now a part of the country's cultural heritage, and as such, controls were needed. China accumulated a seventy-three ton stock pile of ivory to insure a constant supply.

For two-thousand years possessing ivory was a luxury enjoyed by Chinese emperors. The world's newest economic juggernaut created millionaires. Owning ivory was a symbol of upward mobility. The emergence of China's upper class created an unprecedented demand for ivory sculptures.

An ear-splitting blast from the ship's horn signaled the departure of the Flying Dragon. Wei waited until the last mooring-line was castoff to walk down the gangway. A smoke spewing tugboat began to pull the ship away from the wharf. Wei was relieved; the cargo was no longer his responsibility.

Wei dreaded meeting with the head of Mozambique's smuggling syndicate. Duarte was a skinny mulatto in his early thirties. Duarte was never seen in public without his stable of hired criminals. At their last meeting, Wei was taunted mercilessly. Wei chose a popular seaside restaurant for the get-together hoping to avoid his degradation. That hope would go unrealized.

Duarte arrived in a chauffeur-driven black Mercedes. The tinted windows pulsated from rap music. When the doors opened, the exiting passengers were engulfed in a cloud of hashish smoke.

Duarte entered the restaurant surrounded by his entourage. Wei assumed they were armed and on drugs. He was right on both accounts. They gathered around Wei's table. Duarte, puffed up with self-importance, sat down facing Wei. He crossed his arms over his chest. The muscle-bound lout standing behind Wei mocked him by protruding his upper teeth. His charade caused uncontrolled laughter. One larger thug thumped Wei's ear. Wei brushed the man's hand away and cursed him in Mandarin. Wei's annoyance was instantaneously elevated to rage. It was unmistakable that Duarte was enjoying Wei's humiliation.

When he recognized the change in Wei, he ended the mockery by feebly admonishing his gang in Portuguese. Wei placed a satchel of money on the table. "You count money. I very busy man."

"Hey, don't pay any attention to them. They're just having fun. I thought we were gonna party for a few days. I've got the girls, man. C'mon, whatdaya say."

"No time for silly games. You satisfied, I go now."

"Sure Wong, I mean Wei. Anything you say."

As Wei and Duarte parted company their thinking was one and the same. They savored the thought of killing each other.

James Gardner

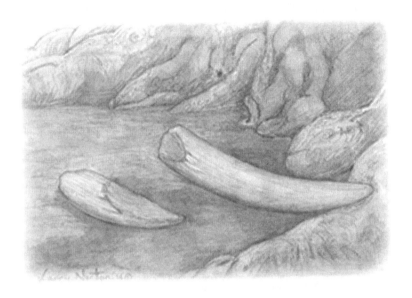

4

Just when it seemed hopeless, Rigby and Jed received word that a trial date had been set.

Their shackles made them shuffle like old men as they were paraded before the court. The manacles were meant more for demeaning than restraining. Rigby smiled at his daughter and grandson as he was helped up into the box of the accused. The black magistrate looked striking in his dark flowing robe and the curly white wig. Rigby Croxford had been fingered as the lone shooter. Jed was viewed as his unarmed accomplice. A guilty verdict was a foregone conclusion, but Rigby's solicitor, Paul Conley, the best legal mind in Zimbabwe, had other plans.

These were the salient points of the trial:

During the initial round of questioning, Rigby denied firing his weapon at Michael Sibanda. He testified that he fired warning shots to prevent the helicopter from leaving what he described as the crime scene. The prosecution claimed that since no animals were recovered; no crime had taken place. Rigby's testimony was corroborated by Jed.

But the court ruled that Jed was a devoted friend and by his own admission would do or say anything to exonerate the accused. Jed's version was ruled inadmissible and stricken from the record.

The prosecutor claimed that it was Croxford's intent to kill Dkari Sibanda's son. And that Michael Sibanda had been stalked and murdered by the accused, Mr. Croxford, who falsely believed the victim's father was responsible for his wife's death. Dr. Helen Croxford's cause of death was ruled to be accidental. This was a clear-cut case of a distraught husband seeking revenge.

More importantly, the prosecution produced eyewitnesses who contradicted Rigby's and Jed's rendition of the gun battle.

Rigby's barrister, Conley, approached the bench and addressed the magistrate. "Sir, the weapon taken from my client was a Winchester .458. This has been the preferred weapon used by elephant hunters in Africa for fifty years." "Make your point, Mr. Conley," demanded the magistrate grimacing as he painfully broke wind.

"A Winchester of that caliber would decapitate a human being, sir. I move that we substitute a baboon as a target to ascertain the effectiveness of the weapon in question. I believe the evidence will prove without a doubt, that a smaller caliber bullet killed Mr. Sibanda."

"Your motion is denied, Mr. Conley. This court wants no part in killing helpless animals. Anything else, sir?"

"Yes, your Honor." He started his motion by discrediting the government's witnesses whom he characterized as known criminals of questionable reputations. The magistrate overruled him. The testimony of the witnesses would be allowed. Conley asked for a ten-minute recess, which the magistrate reluctantly granted.

Ten minutes later the magistrate banged his gavel. "Mr. Conley, are you ready to proceed. I have a full docket."

"My Lord, I know you share my desire for a swift conclusion to these proceedings, but a man's life is at stake here today. I'd like to call each witness one last time, if it pleases the court."

The magistrate readjusted his lopsided wig. "I hope my honorable friend is not wasting the court's time. You may continue with due haste, sir."

Conley produced a large blackboard. He questioned each witness as to their precise location during the firefight. He requested that each man pinpoint his exact position and the direction they fired their respective weapons.

After the last witness had finished testifying, Conley clasped his hands behind his back and addressed the court. "Sir, it has been my experience that in spite of this government's well-publicized deficiencies, our judicial system has remained relatively unbiased and fair. For this, I am proud to call myself a Zimbabwean."

The magistrate stated, "Your patriotism is noted and commendable. Shakespeare wrote, 'Brevity is the soul of wit.' Please make your point expeditiously, sir."

"The witnesses or shall I call them, credible eyewitnesses, testified that everyone, except the victim, Michael Sibanda, faced the accused, Mr. Croxford, during the gunfire exchange. Mr. Croxford is a professional hunter and he is considered an expert marksman, but even he couldn't shoot a man in the face with his back turned. One must conclude that Michael Sibanda was accidentally shot by one of his own men."

The incident in question took place in Matabeleland, the last bastion of opposition to a dysfunctional government. The Shona and the Matabele tribes have a long history of bad blood between them. The majority Shona tribe had brutalized the Matabele tribe for decades.

The court's magistrate, a member of the Matabele tribe, was a locally elected official and therefore not controlled by the government, at least not totally. More importantly, the magistrate's son's life had been saved by the late Dr. Helen Croxford.

The magistrate pounded his gravel. The courtroom quieted. He would delay his final verdict pending a more thorough investigation. Court was adjourned. Rigby and Jed were released under their own recognizance. Cheering erupted. Police cleared the courtroom.

Dkari Sibanda was enraged. He stormed out of the courtroom.

One week later, the poacher who accidentally fired the errant bullet into Michael Sibanda's brain was found murdered. Fearing further retaliation, the remaining poachers fingered the victim as the accidental shooter. The magistrate had no choice. He exonerated Rigby and Jed, with one proviso. They could no longer participate in anti-poaching patrols.

The not-guilty verdict infuriated Dkari Sibanda. An old African proverb says, "There is no honey sweeter than vengeance." Sibanda believed that Rigby Croxford was not only responsible for his son's death; he was threatening his lucrative poaching business. Sibanda would deal with Rigby Croxford on his own terms.

Without Rigby Croxford leading the anti-poaching campaign, Sibanda's trucks lumbered across Zimbabwe to Beira, a coastal seaport in Mozambique, unopposed. Ships destined for China and other Asian ports hauled tons of ivory. Poachers killed hundreds of elephants. Zimbabwe's animal protector had been silenced.

Endangered animals edged closer to extinction.

5

Christine worried about her father. He was lost without his anti-poaching patrols. Inactivity was his nemesis. He wasn't eating properly and his drinking became so excessive even his closest friend, Jedediah, gave him a wide berth. She heard him pacing at night and knew he couldn't sleep. She didn't object when his Matabele trackers pitched his tent overlooking the medical clinic. Every night, from her bedroom window, she watched her father sitting alone by the campfire. When she checked on him in the morning, he hadn't moved.

For Rigby, time didn't heal. If he drank enough gin, he avoided the demons that visited him nightly. The mornings brought him back to his painful reality.

One night, Christine was awakened by her father's intoxicated outburst directed at one of his trackers. His ranting got the dogs barking. That's enough, she thought. It can't go on like this.

As Christine climbed the hill toward her father's tent, she thought about her parents. Her mother had been her role model. But it was her father who bonded together the loose ends of her life. And now, his vulnerability made her feel rudderless.

She'd spent her life worrying about her father. His military experience made him a valued asset for the troubled governments in Africa, which were never in short supply. And there was his work as a professional hunter.

Guns and booze were a bad mix. Living in a lawless country was risky enough. What happened to her mother was proof enough of that.

Ignoring her parents' advice, she married the wrong man. Like most do-gooders, the rawness of Africa took a toll on her American husband. Robert wasn't intended for bush-doctoring. He was better suited as the Park-Avenue gynecologist he became. The marriage ended after only three years. He left her with a son. In the ensuing years, her ex-husband's trips to visit his son became less frequent and then they stopped all together. She stopped to catch her breath. Her father's silhouette was drenched in the campfire's glow. His two Rhodesian ridgebacks lay curled up at his feet. He cradled a bottle of Gordon's gin in his lap.

"What're you waiting for, a roll of the drums? What's up, doc?" he slurred. He rolled the crick out of his neck and flexed his shoulders.

She answered with her hands splayed on her hips. "Well?" Her eyes were taut with unfinished tears, the grief still holding at the corners of her mouth.

Rigby stared into the fire deep in thought, but looked up at the sound of his daughter's voice. He took a swig of gin and muttered, "Well what, love? Enlighten me. I'm riveted with anticipation."

This was how their arguments often started.

She looked through the flames at him. A bat swooping down to catch a moth made her duck. "How can you live like this?" She spread her hands gesturing abhorrence.

He pushed a log in with his foot to feed the fire. "Your mother loved sleeping under the stars. Christine, let's not beat around the bush. Make your damn speech. That's why you're here, isn't it?"

"What on God's green earth are you talking about?" She raised an eyebrow trying to look mystified.

"I'm talking about you trying to stop me. Don't leave out the part about my grandson needing me. And please don't mention God in my presence. I'm stuck someplace between hating God and blaming myself for what happened to your mother." His bloodshot eyes looked painfully sad.

"Mom's death wasn't your fault or anyone else's. It was an accident." She wiped away the tears. "By the way, my son does need you and so do I. Damn you anyway. Drinking yourself to death isn't the answer. What does that prove?"

He looked up and smiled at her drunkenly. "Oh, I don't know. At this point, death doesn't seem so bad."

"Well now, isn't that a lovely solution," she said, watching his face for a reaction.

When he spoke his words were even more garbled. "Christine, you know something, you're just like your mother, an independent woman who tolerates men.

Now me, I'm a man of lesser talents. Fortunately, killing men has been my life's work, and I'm damn good at it. I ought to be good. I've had enough bloody experience—one of the few benefits of a life wasted in Africa. I may have failed your mother in life. I damn sure won't fail her in death."

"That's the gin talking. Mom loved you."

"I know she loved me. But she could have managed without me and so can you. If I find out Dkari Sibanda was implicated in your mother's death, I'll deal with him. End of story. Our friend, Sibanda, is about to meet his maker—the Devil, I reckon. Are we clear on that?"

"Abundantly. I knew this was a waste of time."

"Stay for awhile. Have a little drink, love." He held up the gin bottle as a peace offering.

Christine's lips puckered. "No thanks." She started to leave and then she added as an afterthought, "Oh, I almost forgot. A potential safari client, a woman, stopped by the clinic yesterday."

"Not interested." He caressed the gin bottle. His voice had the I-don't-give-a-shit quality.

"She was adamant about hiring you."

"Tell her I have more pressing issues or whatever you want. I couldn't care less."

"She asked me to tell you her name. Her name is Roth. Lillian Roth."

Her father shot her a bleary glance and resumed his concentration on the dying embers. He appeared transported in time as his memory raced back across the years. Christine waited for an explanation. When none was forthcoming she asked, "You know her?"

He hesitated for a moment. "I knew her from Israel. We worked together on a kibbutz. Lucky for me, Israel accepted white Rhodesian combatants after our war."

His daughter said, "Remember mom saying we had a secret benefactor? How we got that anonymous donation for the clinic? I think it might be her."

He finger-combed his hair and asked, "What makes you say that?"

"Oh, I don't know. Maybe it was by the questions she asked. Anyway, why not ask her in person. She's staying at the Safari Lodge."

He looked at her, reflectively scratching his beard. "I might just do that."

"Be careful, she's stunning. And take a bath. You stink to high heaven."

"My dogs love me." He reached down, picked up a stick and flung it. The youngest ridgeback bounded after it. After retrieving the stick, the dog proudly dropped it at his feet. When he praised the dog, the other one whimpered jealously. Both dogs rolled over presenting their bellies.

She pinched her nose and spoke nasally. "No wonder, you smell like them."

"Goodnight, Dr. Freud. Thanks for the psychobabble and the free hygiene lesson."

She smiled, but quickly smothered it. Their usual repartee had succumbed to sorrow. "Don't mention it," she yelled over her shoulder.

The next morning as Rigby drove to the Safari Lodge, he reminisced about Lillian Roth. The memory evoked infatuation mingled with enough guilt that he erased it from his mind and concentrated on avoiding the deepest corrugations in the washboard road. He looked at himself in the rearview mirror. His hair bore evidence of a comb, but it was still untamed. It was the first time he'd shaved since his wife's death. His face itched from the black soap. He tried unsuccessfully to smooth back his hair. Screw it, he thought.

The Safari Lodge stood out like an oasis in a rock-strewn desert. With rounded ornate gables, the whitewashed Cape Dutch structure topped by a combed grass-thatched roof was reminiscent of houses in the Netherlands. Spindly mango trees burdened by unripened fruit provided shade for a family of kneeling warthogs grazing on the front lawn. Two bleached elephant skulls marked the entrance to a sandstone walkway. Thick white-flowering bougainvillea guarded the red-framed windows. A sprinkler produced a light drizzle of water. Black women weeded the flower beds.

Rigby parked his Land Rover, snubbed out a cigarette and tossed the half-empty pack on the dashboard. As he started for the lobby, he saw a man walking toward him.

He thought about ducking behind his vehicle, but the man had already made eye contact.

"Nice to see you out and about, Croxford," the man said twiddling a tip of his waxed moustache.

"Better to be seen than viewed, I reckon," Rigby said.

"Indeed. Sorry I missed Helen's memorial. Heard it was a fine tribute. Buffalo hunting in the Matesi concession. Good clients are so bloody hard to come by these days. I'm sure you understand. Say, I'm meeting my wife for lunch. Care to join us?"

Rigby ignored the invitation. "So, how was the hunting?"

"Not too bad. Shot a respectable Boone-and-Crockett buffalo." The man digressed. "Heard about your little cock-up with the CID munts. Shocking affair. Glad everything turned out for the best. This government is so bloody useless, wouldn't you agree? I..."

"Oops. Sorry, I'm late for my meeting." Rigby said and added, "Cheers." As he walked away he heard the man mumble to himself, "Poor bugger is lost without his wife."

The African doorman clicked his heels together and saluted. "*Livukile, Bwana.*" The leopard skin draped over his shoulder and a spear made him look like an extra in a Tarzan movie. They had served together in the Rhodesian Bush War. They were old friends.

"Marry anyone lately?" Rigby inquired provocatively.

The doorman smiled until there was no more room on his face. The act reduced his eyes to happy oriental slits. "My wives are old and they cackle like chickens, but they are hard workers. Nowadays, these modern girls are lazy and they are much too costly."

"I'll take that as you're still looking," Rigby noted grinning.

The doorman slapped his thigh and laughed.

The dining room was almost empty. Four African civil servants dressed in cheap business suits conversed loud enough to convey their newfound status. Two tourists and a guide discussed their pending safari. A bartender polished a wineglass. The maitre d' beamed.

Lillian Roth watched Rigby enter the room. Yup, he's just as I remember him, she thought. The square chin and those China-blue eyes verging into grey—the confident gliding gait. A body still defined by hard-earned muscles. He's older, but as handsome as ever. She stood up as he approached the table.

JAMES GARDNER

Lily's gabardine slacks followed the curve of her hips before disappearing into a waspish waistline. Her opened blouse, meant to arouse was a success. The auburn hair, unsullied by grey was styled to look like she had just stepped out a shower. Her unwrinkled face was powdered with sun freckles. The sight of her brought a smile to his face.

"How've you been, Lily?" He stuck out his hand. She ignored the gesture by presenting her cheek, which he kissed. For a split second they were lost in each other's gaze.

"Rigby, you haven't aged one iota."

"You're still as beautiful as ever, Lily."

She said, "Enough with the compliments. Where on earth do we begin?" They said the things they'd saved to tell each other. Their relationship having ended on a sour note made them uneasy. Lillian lessened the awkwardness by delving into the last thirty years. After completing her stint in the Israeli military, she married an American. The short marriage failed. She had one daughter. She built a successful medical device company. Rigby's eyes glazed over as she described her company.

"So, tell me about your daughter? By the way, she's beautiful."

"Christine? She always knew she wanted to be a doctor. Married a dodgy character, which I never let her forget. Divorced, needless to say. Hope she finds someone. Her perfectionism may stand in the way. In truth, I feel privileged having her as a daughter."

"How nice. What about you?" she asked.

"Me? I reckon my CV's rather dull, actually. Always work for soldiering in Africa. I worked in Sierra Leone, Rwanda and the Congo, just to name a few."

"As a mercenary?" she asked.

"In the beginning. Later, behind the scenes," he admitted with a disarmingly self-deprecating grin.

"What was your scariest moment?" she asked.

He thought for a moment and then he said, "Eight-hundred thousand Rwandan Tutsis and Hutus died in six months—hacked each other up with machetes. I ended up right in the middle. It was a bloody horror show. And there was my experience in the Great Congo War—that was a real heart-pumper."

"I never heard of the Congo War."

"You're not alone. As someone once said, 'The darkest thing about Africa has always been our ignorance of it'. As late as the fifteen century, an Italian monk wrote that Africans were three-legged monsters. The lack of knowledge worked both ways. Early on, Africans thought that all white men had one eye. I reckon because they saw white men peering into a looking-glass or down a rifle's sight. About that war, everyone knows that six million Jews died in the holocaust. No one knows or cares about the six million Africans who died in the Great Congo War a few years ago. African wars are always about greed. In this case, conflict diamonds and rare earth minerals."

"Being gassed is different," Lily asserted defiantly.

Rigby countered. "Maybe, but the end result is always the same, the helpless get slaughtered. We, I mean 'we' as a species can be very cruel and our cruelty is transmittable."

"Sometimes, wars are necessary."

"Someone once wrote, 'War is delightful to those who have no part of it'. That pretty well sums up my feelings."

He sensed she wanted him to elaborate on his role in the Rhodesian war, but the memory was too painful. He diverted the conversation. "Anyway, we lost the farm thanks to our legendary president. I worked as a professional hunter for a few years, not by choice, mind you. Now, I'm involved in the wildlife conservation movement."

When his reminiscence evolved to include his wife, Lily interrupted him. "I read about her passing. She must have been a great lady." She squeezed his arm sympathetically.

He acknowledged her compliment with a forced smile. "She was indeed. Not sure why she settled for someone like me."

He wanted to change the subject, but she carried on. "Modesty becomes you, Mr. Croxford." Lily smiled and then she added, "She married the best man I ever knew. The biggest regret of my life was letting you get away. I was young and stupid. Can't believe I just said that. I had this wonderful speech planned." She studied him silently for a few seconds. "For what it's worth, I meant every word." She had allowed him a glimpse of her feelings and looked embarrassed for having done so. Her cheeks blushed rosily.

Lily's flattery made him squirm. The lump in his throat prevented him from answering for a few long seconds. He changed directions again. "Of course there were disappointments. But as someone once said, 'Africa marks the soul with an indelible graffiti.'"

Lily put down her menu. "Sounds like you two had something special." She was envious, but this wasn't about rekindling an old romance; it was about something far more serious. Don't get ahead of yourself, she warned herself. Men are so predictable.

"Refresh my memory. Tell me about your family." she asked.

He told her his grandfather was a civil engineer recruited by Cecil John Rhodes. Rhodes used the diamond concessions he nefariously obtained from the then-king of Matabeleland, Lobengula, to annex what became Rhodesia. Rhodes paid his grandfather in raw land. Later, his father traded that land for what he thought was decent farmland. He should have followed his father's footsteps and stayed with engineering. By his own admission, he wasn't much of a farmer. Against all odds, he managed he eke out living. Having four sons saved him. We helped him turn that godforsaken land into one of the most productive farms in Rhodesia. When the government confiscated my parent's farm it spelled the end. They lost their will to live. Died from broken hearts, I guess you could say."

"What were your brothers' names? What happened to them?"

"Like me, my father worked as a professional hunter for a time. He named his sons after arms companies. There was Smith and Wesson and Remington and of course, yours truly. I own a .375 Rigby, but my weapon of choice is a Winchester.

"Are they still here in Africa?" Lily asked.

"Two live in Australia. One died in the Congo War."

A waiter interrupted him. Mentioning the Congo triggered a flashback. As Lily ordered her lunch, Rigby relived an incident in the Congo War. *He remembered driving around a sharp bend at night. There was a roadblock. Five skinny kids armed with AK-47s stepped out of the darkness. One soldier wanted to shoot the kids on the spot, but he stopped the man. They were so small they needed to use their feet to engage the weapons' receivers. They were high from snorting brown-brown, a mixture of heroin and gunpowder.*

They took our money, my wedding band and my Timex. And then they let us go. He remembered being stopped by rebels and forced to drive back to the scene of the robbery. The five skinny boys were laid out. The back of their heads were missing. The rebel commander returned the money. He apologized for the inconvenience. He kept my Timex. His daydream seemed to last longer, but it was over in a split second.

"Anything wrong?" Lily observed, touching his arm.

"What? No. I'm fine," he said holding her alarmed gaze for a few long seconds.

They talked over poached bream and parsley potatoes. She ordered coffee. He ordered a second glass of wine hoping to lessen his hangover. As he fished for the cigarettes that weren't there, doubts about Lily germinated in the back of his mind. He sensed their meeting wasn't an accident.

"Hope the fish is acceptable," he asked wondering why she was only nibbling at the edges.

Lily's fork stopped halfway to her mouth.

"Mm, it's brilliant." She patted her stomach. "Always fighting the battle."

"Lily, I'd say you've won the war."

She felt blood rushing into her chest making her nipples tingle. After their reunion ran out of steam, he gave her a chance to explain why she was there. When she didn't, he asked, "So, Lily, what brings you to our part of the world?"

"Sorry, I'm not following you."

"Something tells me you're not into wildlife voyeurism. What's the attraction?"

"Is it that obvious?" She dabbed the corners of her mouth with a napkin. "I have something I'd like to show you." She retrieved a manila envelope from underneath the table and fanned herself with it.

"I'll look at it under one condition."

"Hmm. Which is...?" she asked fluttering her long eye lashes.

"That you answer two questions."

The joviality was gone. Her face toughened. "Fair enough, but you're gonna have lots of questions after you see these," she said, sliding the folder across the table. "I apologize for showing you this during lunch. Hope you have a strong stomach. Now, if you'll excuse me, nature calls."

He suppressed the temptation to stare at her as she walked away. Steady, old boy, he warned himself. He opened the folder letting two grainy photographs and a newspaper clipping spill out onto the table. He felt a chill. The hair on the nape of his neck stood up and his arms prickled with gooseflesh. The first photo was of a man on his knees wearing an executioner's hood. Four masked men dressed in black robes stood behind the condemned man. Three were armed with Kalashnikov assault rifles. The fourth man held a long sickle-shaped sword above the man's neck. Their faces were partially hidden behind black scarves. The last photo showed a man's severed head. The beating the man had endured before he was beheaded disfigured his face enough to make him unrecognizable, but the thinning hair said he was an older man. The killers held up their weapons celebrating in the background.

Lily sat down heavily. "Sorry I ruined your appetite."

He held up the last photograph. "I take it you know or rather you knew this one."

"You might say that. I was married to him once upon a time."

"You're kidding."

Her eyes were seriously at work. "I wish. You have no idea how much I wish."

He tossed the newspaper article on top of the photographs. "This wasn't very kind to your ex. Referred to him as one of the most malevolent white-collar criminals in history."

"David ruined people's lives, not to mention what he's done to my daughter. I know this sounds callous, but what happened couldn't have happened to a more deserving person."

Her bluntness shocked him, but he managed to look unaffected. "I'm confused, was he or was he not your daughter's father?"

Lily opened her mouth and put her finger in it, as though she was trying to make herself vomit. "No way. The second biggest regret of my life was marrying David Levy."

"Why show this to me now?" Rigby asked.

"I'll get to that in a minute." She filled in the voids of her life. She married David Levy, when she was thirty. Levy was a Wall-Street lawyer who used her as an Israeli trophy wife to help him gain access to some of the world's most prominent Jewish families. She stayed in Israel. He commuted between New York and Tel Aviv. The long distance marriage failed. Years later, Levy became grotesquely wealthy. After his death, authorities learned that his investment empire was a complete sham. Investors lost billions.

Out of the corner of his eye, Rigby saw the same man he'd met outside and his wife walking toward their table. God damn it, not those gossip mongers. Not now, he thought.

He whispered to Lily, "Don't look up."

The couple wouldn't be deterred. "I say, Croxford, my wife wanted to express her relief about you being exonerated. Hope we're not interrupting anything serious."

The woman stepped forward and patted Rigby's shoulder with her boney hand. She frowned at Lily who returned a sickly smile. The woman's vinegary look said, how could you, his wife just died. She was about to speak when Lily cut her off. Without introducing herself, Lily grabbed the woman's hand roughly and announced, "I'm hiring Mr. Croxford to investigate my late husband's murder. Lily retrieved the photograph of her dead ex-husband and placed it on the table. The woman pressed her hand over her mouth and gasped. She leaned against her husband for support. "Dear God in heaven, how awful. We're so sorry we interrupted you. Please excuse us." Nothing was said to lessen their embarrassment. They walked away without looking back.

Rigby waited until they were out of earshot. "Well done, Lily."

Undeterred, Lily asked, "What did that man mean when he said you were exonerated?"

"Oh, that. I was brought up on criminal charges."

"Just out of curiosity, what were the charges?"

"Nothing too serious, just murder," he replied with a faint smile. "I was found not guilty."

Lily shook her head. "You must be relieved."

"Quite." Quickly, he redirected the topic as he reexamined the photographs. "Why get involved now. This happened months ago?"

"Because my daughter was with him when he was abducted."

"What makes you think she's still alive? Oops. I shouldn't have said that." He touched her shoulder seeking forgiveness. Referring to the photographs again, he asked, "I assume these were taken someplace in the Middle East?"

"No, here in Africa. North Africa to be precise. I received this two weeks ago." She handed him a handwritten note. "It was written by my daughter and it was posted from Mombasa, Kenya. My ex-husband was cruising on his sailboat dolling out money to African charities. His contrition for the crimes he committed, I suppose. They were boarded off Djibouti or thereabouts. The fact that he was one step ahead of the law and that he embezzled the money only came out later. For some reason, David reestablished contact with his stepdaughter. He wasn't very kind to her during our marriage. In fact it was almost like a male lion killing a cub to get the lioness to come into season. I'm sure you can relate. I mean about the lions. Anyway, never knowing her real father made her receptive. I had my suspicions, but, fool that I am I kept them to myself."

"My Hebrew's a bit rusty. What's it say?"

"Basically, that she's alive." Lily remarked.

"Any mention of ransom?"

"It contains something only my daughter could have written. Nothing about ransom."

He guessed the answer but pressed her anyway. "I still don't see why you've involved me?"

"I know about that rescue you led in the Sudan a few years back. Rigby, I swear I wouldn't be asking for your help if there was any other way."

He picked at a razor scab on his neck. "I'm afraid it's not quite that simple."

She made a questioned face. "Oh. In what way?"

"What took place in the Sudan happened ten years ago. Truth be known, that rescue was compromised from the start. I ended up in the middle of a genocidal civil war. People who deserved better died. And another thing, the Sudan is like France compared to North Africa. I mean, we're talking about murderers and rapists and they're the nice guys. The region is a human-cesspool of depravity."

"It can't be that bad."

He checked the scab for blood. "If the world had one toilet, it would be in North Africa."

Lily's resolve couldn't be diverted. "But you found the American you were hired to rescue."

"Well, yes. Look, in case you haven't noticed, I'm not as young as I used to be. I'm not ready for an old folk's home, but..."

"Nonsense, you turned sixty December fifth. That's not old." She stared at him defiantly.

He was surprised she remembered his birthday. He leaned forward and steepled his hands. "That may not be old for some things, but it is for what you need. Bloody hell, that didn't come out right. You know what I'm trying to say."

His double entendre pinkened her cheeks. "About the questions I agreed to answer."

"I've always been curious. Why did you send me packing forty years ago? One minute, I thought we were getting married, and the next thing I knew I was on a plane flying back to South Africa." He spoke with a touch of irony in his voice.

"Funny, that's not how I remember it." She paused daring him to disagree, when he didn't she said, "When I asked you to consider converting to my religion, you said all religions were the superstitious inventions of simple-minded men."

"To tell you the truth, I don't remember using those exact words. I do believe most religious types are weak people trying to prolong their pitiful lives. When I hear Gabriel's horn, I plan on going quietly. But then again, I'm not on speaking terms with God at the moment."

"For whatever reason, you walked out of my life in a huff," she said.

"In my defense, the violence I witnessed in the war affected me in ways you never understood. If you remember, I did lose my best friend and for that matter, my country."

She shook her head disagreeing. "I'm an Israeli—we're not strangers to violence. The thing is, eventually I understood everything, but it was too late for us." She explained that she had loved him, but she couldn't disappoint her parents. They were holocaust survivors who opposed an interfaith marriage. The horrors they endured contaminated their lives.

They existed in a state of forced neutrality, unable to feel or show affection. She was their only child. After their deaths, she realized she'd helped them become professional victims and that they used their suffering to control her life.

"Look at it this way, if it weren't for me, you wouldn't have married Helen."

"It was great for me. Helen deserved better."

She leaned forward and looked squarely into his eyes. "I would've changed places with her in a minute."

Not unnaturally, he was flattered. He acknowledged her compliment by raising his wine glass. The discomforting stalemate was interrupted by his second question. "Lily, did you make a donation to my wife's medical clinic?"

"It wasn't me, it was my daughter."

"What prompted her?"

"That's a long story. By the way, her name is Sarah, like in the Old Testament."

Rigby scrutinized her face. He knew he was missing something. "There are circumstances surrounding Helen's death you need to know." He elaborated on the evidence linking Dkari Sibanda to his wife's death.

As Lily listened she seemed preoccupied. "I take it you've gone to the proper authorities?"

He cleared his throat, looked over both shoulders and whispered, "Authorities? That's a laugh. It doesn't work like that in this country. Make no mistake about it, if Sibanda was implicated, I'll sort him."

"What's the connection with this man again?" she asked.

"Dkari Sibanda's a bigwig in Zimbabwe politics. The Minister of Finance, to be more specific. Helen believed he was, or rather is involved in the illegal wildlife trade. No telling how many millions he's stashed in Swiss bank accounts. She even denounced him publicly." He looked solemn. "Odds are he orchestrated her so-called 'accident'."

"When you say wildlife trade, you mean poaching?"

"Elephants for the ivory and rhino horn for God-knows-what. China's destroying Africa's wildlife. The sad part is the world doesn't give two shits. Pardon my French."

She shook her head. "It's depressing."

"Very," he agreed and continued, "Sibanda's just the tip of the iceberg. The corruption goes all the way to the top. And they're in bed with the Chinese."

"Isn't China building roads and schools here in Africa?"

"A deception perpetrated by their propagandists. Don't get me started. China is gobbling up Africa's natural resources. Africans are so busy killing each other over the table scraps—they can't see the endgame. When everything's gone, the parasite will discard the host."

"What got you involved with conservation?"

"It was Helen's idea." Rigby explained that rhino horn was more valuable than gold. Poachers had recently killed over a thousand rhinos in South Africa. He concluded by predicting the rhino's extinction in ten years. "For me, destroying Africa's wildlife is unacceptable. Does that make any sense?"

"It makes all the sense in the world. Any light at the end of the tunnel?"

"The American government might make it illegal to import animal trophies. It's a small step in the right direction." The beginnings of a smile curled the edges of his mouth. A certain minster heading for extinction had crossed his mind. "That phony murder charge I told you about. It was Dkari Sibanda's son. Accidentally shot by one of his men. I caught them poaching elephants. I mean to sort Sibanda before he does the same to me."

Lily wouldn't be put off. She reminded him that Sibanda wasn't going anywhere, but her daughter's life could be hanging in the balance. Lily searched Rigby's face. When she saw his interest waning, she dropped a bombshell. "What if I told you Sarah isn't just my daughter, she's our daughter?" His jaw dropped. She knew she had his undivided attention. She had opened the door and had to step through it very carefully.

Lily's expression reinforced her claim. Stunned silence ensued. It took time for him to weigh the implications of what she was saying. He had trouble coagulating a denial. Rigby stared at her without speaking. Finally, gritting his mental teeth he stuttered, "Lily, I'd say you're clutching at straws." He tried to look unconvinced.

A prolonged sip of wine gave him time to think. When he put the glass down he inadvertently placed it on top of his fork. "Bumbling idiot," he said of himself. Lily pushed back from the table. He crooked his finger at their waiter who rushed forward and sopped up the spilt wine with a towel. The wine steward produced another glass and an unopened bottle of Chardonnay. "Forget the wine. Bring me a gin and bitters. Better yet, make it a double."

"Make mine the same," Lily said.

"When did you start drinking? I never knew," he observed.

"I could write a book about what you don't know about me. Forty years is a long time."

Lily waited until they were alone. "Look, I don't blame you for being skeptical. I didn't know I was pregnant when you left Israel. I swear on my parents' graves, you're Sarah's father."

Outwardly, he appeared calm, but inside his gut churned. He muffled a painful burp. He snapped out of his confusion blurting, "Good God, Lily, you really are desperate."

"Figured you might have that reaction, I know I would if I were you." She rummaged her purse for a photograph of her daughter and then she slid it across the table.

Rigby examined the photograph from different angles. It was as if he was looking at a mirror image of his daughter, Christine. The doubt in his eyes was still there, but it was less evident now. He unwittingly twisted his wedding band. "I...I don't know what to say. I really don't."

"Oddly enough, like Christine, she's wanted to be a doctor. Sarah had the smarts. I couldn't get her to apply herself." It was the standard lament used by parents of unsuccessful children. Lily continued, "The resemblance is amazing, isn't it? You must be overwhelmed. You were right about one thing, I am desperate." After a few more beats of excruciating quiet she said, "Maybe this wasn't such a good idea after all. I would never have involved you if your wife...." She stood up, her face tight with regret and started to leave. She'd tweaked his sense of honor, it was almost imperceptible, but she knew she'd touched a raw nerve. "It was great seeing you, Rigby."

He pulled back her chair. "Sit down, Lily."

She concealed her elation and complied. "You don't have to do this. No really, I mean it."

"There's a possibility she might already be...." The last word lodged in his throat. He snapped his fingers at the waiter requesting a refill. Absentmindedly, he reached for his cigarettes again. "Like I said, the note could have been written months ago."

"She's alive," Lily stated adamantly and added, "Don't ask me how I know, I just do."

"Yes, of course. How much, if anything, does Sarah know about me?

Lily told him that Sarah had always known about him. As a child she fantasized about meeting her real father, but disrupting Rigby's life was never an option. Lily showed him a tattered photograph. It was a close-up of Rigby and Lily on a beach. His tee-shirt bore the Selous Scout emblem.

Lily pointed at the insignia saying, "Sarah always referred to you as her eagle."

"Not that it matters. It's not an eagle, it's an osprey. Do you know where she was when she wrote this note? You would think Israeli intelligence would lend a hand. I mean, you are Israeli citizens."

"Someplace in the Gulf of Tadjoura—north of Djibouti City. As far as Israeli intelligence goes, they've ignored me. I'm not sure why. For whatever reason, I've virtually been on my own."

"It sounds like they're headed south." The question is, how far south, he thought.

Lily leaned forward in her chair. "What're you thinking?"

"I led counterinsurgency coastal raids during the Eritrean Civil War. By and large, arms interdictions."

"So, you know the coast?" Lily asked.

"For all intents and purposes, yes. Was she still onboard her stepfather's yacht?"

Again there was a pause before she answered. "She didn't say."

"Just out of curiosity, what's the yacht's name?"

"The Black Cygnet. It vanished without a trace. She's over twenty meters."

He doodled on a frosted water glass with his finger. "Hard to hide a yacht that size, you would think."

Lily said, "Scuttled her, no doubt. His mother ship, the Black Swan, is over a hundred meters. She was seized in the Greek Islands. Like I said, my ex-husband was a very accomplished crook."

Rigby picked up the snapshot of the executioner holding up Lily's ex-husband's severed head. Beyond the obvious, there was something about the picture that troubled him. He couldn't put his finger on it and then a light went off in his head. He recognized a faded tattoo on the executioner's forearm. It was a copy of a Special Forces combat badge, the bottom half of a human skull with a dagger protruding from its jaw. Well, I'll be damned—this one is a Yank. He started to tell Lily, but didn't. He appeared to be miles away tapping his lips with his forefinger and then drumming the table.

"Hey, are you listening to me?" She placed her hand on his arm. He freed himself and checked for onlookers. Her green eyes twinkled with mischief.

After staring into his drink for a long moment, then he said, "Avidly." He blinked regaining his focus. "Huh, sorry, I was just thinking. That part of Africa doesn't have functioning governments. Warlords run the show. That might work in our favor."

"Does this mean you're gonna help me?" She wet her fingers with her lips and then she attempted to smooth out his hair. The attention made him squirm, which appeared to please her.

"Yes," Rigby said thoughtfully. "C'mon Lily, you knew I could never say 'no' to you."

So far, it had all gone as she planned. Lily allowed herself the thinnest of smiles trying not to appear as victorious as she felt. "There was something else in Sarah's note you need to hear. She said and I quote, 'I need my eagle.'"

The questions and speculations swirled around in his head. He felt a tinge of affection for the daughter he never knew. Is she telling the truth or is she playing me, he asked himself. For the moment, he buried his doubt. "The first order of business is to get you checked out of this ungodly expensive hotel. We're gonna need all the cash we can get our hands on. Bribery is an art form in Africa."

"Not to worry. That medical company I told you about. I have four hundred employees. Money won't be a problem. I'll spend whatever it takes to get Sarah back."

"Right, that's it, then. You need to checkout anyway. Africans have big ears. From now on, we need absolute secrecy. Our lives will be at risk. You need to know that going in."

"How's your daughter going to handle this?" she asked quietly.

"Let me worry about Christine."

James Gardner

6

Christine was between rounds at the medical clinic. She looked over her silver-rimmed half-moons at her father and then at Lily. She took off the glasses and placed them on the windowsill. She rubbed the bridge of her nose. I thought I said to go see her, not bring her home with you, she said to herself.

Rigby approached his daughter leaving Lily alone on the veranda. "Doc, this has been a helluva day for me, to say the least. I could use your indulgence."   As Christine listened, she looked puzzled. When he stopped speaking, she shook her head. He put his hands in his pockets and shifted his weight back and forth. The idea of having a sister was appealing to an only child, but there were questions that needed answers. "Hold on, back up a minute. Where's her daughter. Why isn't she here?"

"Well, this is where it gets a bit cheeky." As he outlined the abduction and Lily Rosen's plea for his help, he watched his daughter's smile melt into frown.

Her tone became testy. "Are you seriously suggesting…?"

"I know you're disappointed in me. In fairness, what happened was over forty years ago."

"I'm not disappointed. I am a doctor. As they say in medicine, 'shit happens'. What's disappointing is you seem in a hell of a hurry to get yourself killed."

"But this is what I was trained to do. And if I don't help her, who will?"

"No, this is what you were trained to do forty years ago," she said.

"I can still handle myself." He puffed himself up. Holding his breath caused an untimely coughing jag. He stubbed the cigarette out on his heel and stuck the half-smoked butt behind his ear. "Perhaps, you should ask yourself, what if your son got pinched." He hacked from the depths of his lungs, but pretended to clear his throat.

Christine paddled the lingering smoke. She retrieved the butt and dropped it into a wastepaper basket as if it were a radioactive dog turd. "Mom said you were an anachronistic warrior in search of a cause. Let's be honest, Lily's problem is perfect for you."

He coughed before he spoke again. "My, aren't you the know-it-all."

Two vertical wrinkles deepened her forehead. Her mouth formed an irritated sneer. "I don't claim to know everything, but I do know you. I'm curious. Any other revelations you wanna get off your chest?"

He eyed the dustbin mourning the discarded cigarette. "I guess that's everything."

"I know you've already made up your mind, so anything I say is a waste of time. Don't just stand there, go get her."

"Doc, when you rein in the bitchiness, you really are quite fetching." He blotted the beads of perspiration on her forehead with his sleeve and then he hugged her. She playfully extracted herself from his embrace. At least now you have a reason to sober up. And I have time to talk you out of this insanity, she thought.

Rigby motioned to Lily who stepped forward. Christine broke the ice by grabbing Lily's hand. "So, he found you or you found him or something along those lines."

"May I call you Christine or would you prefer Doctor?" Lily asked. "I like to be called Lily by my friends. I hope we can be friends."

Christine nodded without enthusiasm. "Christine is fine. I don't see why we can't be friends."

Lily said, "I know how difficult this must be for you."

Christine's eyebrows knitted. "How so?"

"I mean having your world turned upside down."

"Perpetual chaos is the norm around here. And having him for a father has proven to be, shall I say a life full of surprises."

Rigby gave Lily and his daughter space. They seemed to forge a temporary truce. The sticking point for Christine was that Lily was involving her father in something that could get him killed. She had just lost her mother. The thought of losing her father was too gut-wrenching to imagine.

Later that night, as Rigby studied a coastal map of Africa, he considered the logistics of a rescue effort. He could drive to the Indian Ocean in three days. There were lots of expatriated Rhodesians living in Mozambique who would help him. Possessing firearms was a crime in Zimbabwe, but as a professional hunter he was exempt from the law. The problem was crossing international borders. If he got caught smuggling a weapon it meant serious prison time or worse. Posing as a safari hunting guide might work, and bribing the border guards had worked before. If he could secure a boat, he could cruise along the African coastline gathering intelligence.

Sailing close to the shoreline might lure the same men who kidnapped Lily's daughter, but that was a long shot at best. He checked the distance and realized there was a time problem. He decided to discuss the drawback with Lily in the morning.

As he was preparing for bed, his daughter knocked softly on the half-opened door and then closed it quietly behind her. She sat down on the edge of his bed. "You called me a know-it-all. At the expense of giving you more evidence, if you think this woman's only interested in finding her daughter, you are very naïve, Daddy Dearest."

"What are you talking about?" he asked stifling a yawn that his daughter imitated.

"You know exactly what I mean."

He swallowed drily. "Why, I haven't the foggiest idea."

"Lily means to have you as her next husband."

"Rubbish."

"Dear God, I do believe you've lost the plot. This proves without a doubt that gin diminishes brain cells."

"So indelicately put, me lady." He smiled and then the humor vanished. He showed her his wedding ring. "I'll go to my grave wearing this."

She rested her head on his chest. He stroked strands of hair from her face. Unspent tears welled up in her eyes. She knuckled them out. It took her a few moments to gather her emotions. "Why didn't I marry someone like you?" she asked looking up at him.

He winked down at her. "I reckon because perfection is so rare these days."

"You're impossible." She snickered and then muffled the sound with her hand. She got up and tiptoed to the door. Her voice dropped to barely a whisper. "Sleep tight." She closed the door behind her.

It was the first night he'd gone to bed sober in months. In spite of his attempt to direct his dreaming, a reoccurring vision appeared.

I was visiting a friend's farm in South Africa. The Rhodesian Bush War was winding down. The white minority was losing. The black majority had declared a premature victory. I saw Helen standing alone on the porch looking up at a star-peppered sky. Wispy clouds floated lazily in front of a waxing moon.

I stood in the shadows watching her. Moonshine illuminated the most beautiful face I'd ever seen. I walked up and stood next to her. "It's lovely, isn't it?"

"So many stars," she gushed.

"No, I mean the silence. I'm Rigby Croxford." I extended my hand.

"I'm Helen...."

I interrupted her. "I know who you are. I also know you're a Peace Corps volunteer."

"And you're in the Rhodesian military," she said. "Will the war end soon?"

"For all practical purposes, the hostilities are concluded. The communists won."

"You sound bitter, Mr. Croxford."

I shot her a steely glance. "You're bloody right, I'm bitter. The whole world turned their backs on us. So, let's see how they like having the Russians and the Chinese running Africa."

"According to what I read, the war was a lost cause from its inception. In your opinion, can black Africans ever govern themselves?" she asked rhetorically.

"I reckon they could," I slurred. And then I added, "When pigs fly."

"Ian Smith, your Prime Minister, says blacks won't be ready to rule Rhodesia for a thousand years. Not much of a ringing endorsement."

"I used to worry that God wouldn't forgive us for what we've done to these people."

"And now?" she asked.

"Now? Now, I don't give a rat's ass."

"I find that rather depressing," she said.

"Bleeding heart liberals come to Africa with the best intentions. They go home either clueless or disillusioned or both. You see Africans as paragons of primeval innocence."

Her eyes grew angry. "And how do you see them?"

"As cannibalistic sharks feeding on their own kind," I replied.

"Mr. Croxford, on that point, I think I'll call it a night. Maybe we can resume our conversation when you're in a more civil mood."

I remember knocking a bug off her shoulder. She looked startled and stepped back. Out of the blue, I blurted, "We're going to be married someday." I don't know why I said it.

"Excuse me? What on earth are you talking about?" Her eyes darted.

"I know this sounds crazy, but our future is together."

"Mr. Croxford, either you've had far too much to drink or you're suffering from some sort of battle fatigue. I'll say one thing. You are without a doubt the strangest man I've ever met."

That dream merged into a nightmare.

The sunrise gave the eastern sky a pinkish glow. I looked through my rifle scope zeroing in on a rhino. I had no intention of pulling the trigger, but the Winchester accidentally discharged. It wasn't a kill shot. The bellowing Rhino struggled to stand up.

The image jolted him awake. It took him a while to get his bearings. He got out of bed, walked over to an open window and sat down on the sill. He rubbed the vestiges of sleep from his eyes and lit a cigarette. A cool breeze was scented by night-blooming jasmine. The distant giggling of hyenas momentarily silenced the crickets. His ridgebacks cocked their heads.

As he peered into the darkness, he reviewed the things he wished he'd told his wife. Now it was too late. He vowed not to make the same mistake with Christine. His daughter's insights were a damn nuisance. She was right. Helping Lily is right up his alley, but not for the reason she imagined, at least not entirely. He didn't have the heart to tell Lily that her daughter was, in all probability, already dead. That part of Africa was a haven for kidnappers. The lack of a ransom demand wasn't total confirmation, but the evidence pointed in that direction. There was another reason for helping Lily. Leaving the country would give Dkari Sibanda a false sense of security. He needed Sibanda to drop his guard. Killing him would be difficult, but not impossible. Abducting Sibanda and having him confess was so much more appealing.

JAMES GARDNER

7

One year earlier
New York City

To say David Levy looked like a bullterrier would have offended members of the American Kennel Club. In spite of a fortune spent on plastic surgery, Levy remained a very unattractive person. His appearance had many more failures than successes. The facial skin had been stretched so tight, spider webs of red capillaries crisscrossed his cheeks. Hair transplants made an atrocious comb-over look too symmetrical—like a furrowed field of planted corn. Two facelifts had given him droopy polar-bear eyes. A second rhinoplastic procedure produced a Michael-Jackson nose. Levy was a small man with a large appetite for finer things.

Levy examined himself in an antique mirror. He furled back his upper lip and checked his teeth and his nostrils. He dusted an errant flake of dandruff from the lapel of his Desmond Merrion suit. Satisfied with his appearance, he moved to a picture window with a view of the Hudson River. Crumbling redbrick warehouses and abandoned factories lined the far side of the river. Below his office, limousines delivered the movers-and-shakers of Wall Street. Stock traders hurried to make the opening bell of the New York Stock Exchange. Impatient horn blowers and the distant wail of a police siren made the morning sound ordinary.

As the founding director of Global Investments, an investment firm managing over twenty billion dollars in assets, David Levy was responsible for adherence to regulations defined by the Sarbanes-Oxley Act. This was the last day of an audit conducted by the Securities Exchange Commission. His firm had never failed an SEC audit. What was different this time was that Levy's lavish lifestyle was placing unsustainable demands on the firm's resources. As the outflow of misappropriated funds grew, so did the cost of the cover-up. This audit would be as choreographed as any Broadway musical.

David Levy never intended to become a crook. He was the valedictorian of his senior class at a prestigious New England prep school. He even graduated from Harvard Law School. His old colleagues at Solomon Brothers characterized Levy as a stock trader of incredible market savvy. When he started his own firm, investors lined up to open accounts. For the first five years, his investment performance was dazzling. Complacency and market setbacks led to some temporary borrowing from a few unsuspecting clients. Levy's fantasy of repaying the loans faded with time. The impermanent loans became permanent. David Levy, the acclaimed financial genius, was now a common thief.

The intercom buzzed. It was time to hear the SEC's audit evaluation. Levy stood up as his secretary led the auditors into his office. Jacquelyn Atkinson or Jackie as she preferred to be called, with two-year tenure, was the senior auditor. She was an attractive woman in her mid-thirties—a solid eight by anyone's standards.

Her Staten Island accent had been moderated by four years at Duke in Durham, North Carolina. She was one of those unpopular girls in high school nobody ever remembers. She was a little overweight, too smart, poorly dressed and had a proclivity for saying the wrong thing at the wrong time. She was a nerd, to put it mildly.

Jackie's saving grace was that she was a late bloomer. When she attended her ten-year high school reunion, her classmates were dumfounded. It was a stunning transformation. The wallflower of Jefferson High looked like a movie star. Girls who couldn't remember her name now hated her. The boys couldn't believe they let her get away.

Atkinson's assistant, Terrance Cassidy, was well over six feet with a distinctly Celtic cleft chin, an Irish pug-nose, a chiseled jaw and cobalt-blue eyes. Most women found him attractive. The cheap suit and the scuffed wingtips said he was either right out of college or broke or both, as was the case. His most outstanding feature was that behind the horn-rimmed glasses he wore to appear bookish prowled the eyes of a man unencumbered by complex thoughts. Always pressed for funding, the SEC couldn't be choosey.

Terrance Cassidy was raised in Indiana. He was the only boy in a catholic litter of seven. His father owned a farm equipment dealership. He was a wealthy businessman who had a fondness for whiskey and other weaknesses of the flesh. Terry's doting mother spoiled him, as did his six sisters. He could do no wrong. Terry was a slacker.

Terry was the best shooting guard in Indiana. Basketball is a religious movement in the Midwest.

His father's lifelong dream was to watch his son play for Notre Dame in South Bend. That dream would have been realized had Terry not received the lowest SAT scores in the history of Saint James Academy. Mr. Cassidy railed, "Son, you're a disgrace. If you ever do get a job, it'll be one with your name stitched on a work-shirt."

"Leave the boy alone," Mrs. Cassidy said. The girls rallied behind their mother. "Mom's right."

Not to be outfoxed, Terry asked to retake the SATs. This time he paid a fellow classmate, Sol Fishman, to take the test for him in a neighboring county. Solly, who was headed to Yale in the fall, took his clandestine assignment a little too seriously. His SAT score doubled Terry's first attempt. Notre Dame smelled a rat. The University of Kentucky smelled a national championship. As the head of admissions said, "If the kid can sign his name and count to ten, he'll make a fine addition to the student body. Anyone who can dribble with both hands and average twenty-five a game can't be an idiot."

To near universal dismay, Terrance Cassidy not only earned an undergraduate degree, he graduated from the law school. His transformation was just as stunning as Jackie's.

To put the auditors at ease, Levy initiated small talk. Atkinson and Cassidy listened intently as Levy gave his assessment of the current state of the economy. When he sensed they were losing interest, he got down to business. "So, how did we fare? Would either of you like a cup of coffee?" Levy's eyes traveled up and down Atkinson's body, pausing at her beasts.

"No thanks, Mr. Levy."

"Nothing for me," Cassidy also indicated.

"Are you sure? Kopi Luwak is the most expensive coffee in the world." He explained that Indonesians covet coffee beans that have passed through the intestinal tract of a specialized civet cat. Jackie's nose wrinkled. Cassidy grimaced and shook his head.

Jackie said, "Everything at Global seems to be in order notwithstanding a few minor infractions. Nothing that can't be corrected. Please give this to your compliance officer."

JAMES GARDNER

She nodded at Cassidy who placed some stapled sheets on Levy's desk and pushed them forward. "There is one more piece of business. We'd like to see the monthly statements of these five accounts. As you know, it's the agency's policy to randomly select and review individual accounts." She nodded at Cassidy who produced a list of the account numbers.

"Not a problem," Levy said. Before he could comply with her request, his telephone rang. Instead of picking up the receiver, he pushed on the loudspeaker button and then unsuccessfully fumbled with the volume control. "Sir, sorry to interrupt, I've got Senator Schuman on the line." His secretary sounded panicky, but it was play-acting.

"What can I do for you, senator?" Levy muffled the loudspeaker. He carried on a five minute one-sided fictitious conversation with a dead telephone receiver. Schuman was a powerful member on the senatorial banking committee. The theatrical demonstration was designed to impress the auditors.

A man with powerful friends in the government was less likely to be seen as a lawbreaker. It was of course totally irrational, but highly effective.

Levy hung up the receiver. "I apologize. Damn politicians think they're the most important people in the world. They forget who's paying their salaries. Where was I? Oh, yes." He buzzed his secretary. She stepped into his office. He handed her the list of account numbers. "Make photocopies of these statements for our friends." In truth, he didn't need photocopies. He'd secretly received the account numbers hours ago. The monthly statements would be as fictitious as the telephone call he'd just fabricated.

"Are we done?" Levy asked them before his secretary left the room.

"I can't think of anything else. Unless something unforeseen comes up, we should finish our work by the end of the day." Jackie stood up and reached over to shake Levy's hand. Cassidy also got up, but then he raised a finger indicating one more question. He eased himself back down into the chair. Jackie looked irritated, but there was nothing she could do but follow suit. Her brow knitted with annoyance.

Levy made a mental note. The way Atkinson and Cassidy avoided eye contact told him that either they were involved now or they had been in the past. "Fire away, Mr. Cassidy."

Referring to some scribbled notes, Cassidy said, "Sir, I'm curious about your commodity hedge fund division.

I noticed that in the quarter just ended your firm had a significant number of account closures and that the accounts suffered some pretty substantial losses. Are the losses and the attrition normal?"

"Normal is such a subjective term. Trading commodities is complex, and not without risk, I might add. It's all carefully defined in our prospectus. In spite of doing the required due diligence, we sometimes fail to qualify our investors. They fill out the appropriate risk profiles, but some individuals can't stomach the equity swings. It's a shame, really. If they would only stay the course, we'd make them money. I can show you some of our successful accounts."

"That won't be necessary," Jackie said intervening. "Oh, before I forget, I'm being transferred to Washington."

"A promotion, I hope?" Levy looked despondent by the sudden turn of events. He smoothed back a few lonely strands of his comb-over.

"As a matter of fact, it is," Jackie replied.

"Will you be taking her place?" Levy asked Cassidy hopefully.

"Me? No, I'm afraid not. I just passed the New York bar. Next Friday is my last day."

"Congratulations. Just out of curiosity, how long were you employed at the SEC?"

"Six months, give or take."

"Seems like a rather sudden career move," Levy noted.

His mind went into overdrive. Is this my overactive imagination or is something fishy going on.

"I guess you could think of it that way. Truth is, I took the bar exam three times. If I failed it one more time, I was destined for a life as a bean counter. Not that there's anything wrong with counting beans." Cassidy grinned at Jackie seeking exculpation.

"What kind of law will you be practicing?" Levy inquired.

"I'll be working for the city's district attorney." When Cassidy noticed the suspicion in Levy's eyes intensify he threw him a red herring. "I should've gone to work for you, Mr. Levy."

Levy's expression was unrevealing. He felt his stomach lurch, but he acted indifferent. "Well, I wish you much success. I know you'll both do great things. The cream always rises to the top, as someone once said." Levy stood up indicating they should leave, which they did.

As soon as the auditors exited his office, Levy called Andre and recorded the following message:

Your services are no longer needed. Unfortunately, our friend, Miss Atkinson, has been transferred to Washington. Bonus check is in the mail. No need to return her phone calls or mine. Stay well, my friend. I'll be in touch.

As insurance, Levy switched to an untraceable cell phone.

He took the following preliminary precautions: His private jet, a Falcon 2000, would be flown from the Teterboro Airport to an uncontrolled airfield in Atlantic City, New Jersey. As another diversion, he ordered the captain of his three-hundred foot megyacht, The Black Swan, to leave her anchorage at Saint Tropez on the French Riviera and head for the Greek Islands. His sixty foot sloop, The Black Cygnet, would set sail for Ashdod, Israel. Baiting his pursuers to follow the Black Swan was an integral part of the escape plan.

The millions he'd contributed to both candidates in the upcoming presidential election and the current administration spelled the possibility of a presidential pardon. And if he ended up in Israel, the money he'd given to Jewish charities would hopefully slowdown any extradition proceedings. Levy believed his political ties made him untouchable. He just needed time. His temporary disappearance could be the best option. If needed, his vanishing act could be fully implemented in ten days.

It was nine o'clock. Jackie Atkinson was frantic. She'd booked her usual room near the LaGuardia Airport for her weekly rendezvous with Andre. This was the night she'd picked to end her affair, but alcohol was dampening her resolve. She poured herself another vodka and soda and redialed his number. Where is he?

Why isn't he returning my calls? Maybe there's been an accident. These thoughts blurred the realization that loomed in the back of her mind. She knew Andre wasn't coming. That reality made her feel as used as her motel room.

Terry Cassidy was holding court at his favorite Manhattan watering hole, O'Neal's Wake. He twirled his finger indicating another round for the table. His roommate stood up and made a toast. "Here's to the new assistant district attorney." His roommate's girlfriend seconded the toast with, "And to the future mayor of the greatest city in the world."

Cassidy cautioned them. "One small step for justice, but a giant step for yours truly." They clinked glasses. Cassidy drained two fingers of Bullet's bourbon and chased it with a swig of Harps. He smacked the shot-glass on the bar, belched and excused himself.

The men's room smelled like disinfectant and urinated beer. *This has been a hell of a day for me, but something doesn't feel right,* he thought wistfully. *He'd launched his law career without a flaw. Giuliani started his career with the DA, why not me. Things couldn't have worked out better. Best of all, that flimflamming cocksucker, David Levy, was going to prison.*

Then why do I feel so shitty, he asked himself. He stood in front of the urinal thinking about Jackie Atkinson. *No one deserves to go through the shit-storm that's brewing, especially her. She might be naïve, but she didn't have a dishonest bone in her body. Push comes to shove, I'll testify in her behalf. Sure, why not.*

As he stood there looking in the mirror his feelings for her washed over him in waves. *You can't leave well enough alone, can you,* he asked himself.

Jackie Atkinson had polished off two Smirnoff miniatures and was struggling to open a third one when she heard someone knock. She leapt off the bed, ran to the door and jerked it open.

Her warm, sexy smile amended into a disappointed scowl. "What do you want?"

"We need to talk," Cassidy demanded.

"Talk about what?" Her eyes stayed glued on his face.

"Okay, for starters, how about me saving your career."

"Look, I'm not in the mood for whatever you've got in mind. Don't get me wrong, I'm flattered—I'm just not interested." She tried to shut the door, but he used his foot as a doorstop.

"He's not coming."

"Who?" she asked. Her cheeks flushed pink.

"You know who. The man..." He bit off the last words. Even with a first-rate education, Jackie never suspected that Andre was being paid to bed her. There were a few moments of embarrassing silence as she let what he was inferring sink in. "I can help you, Jackie. Now, let me in or I walk. You have no idea of the shit you've stepped in."

She opened the door, walked over and flopped down on the tousled bed. She folded her arms over her chest and hiccupped. "This better be good."

"What's your read on David Levy?" Cassidy asked.

Rather than wait for her answer he opened the mini-bar, grabbed a can of Heinekens and chugged it until the last ounce of foam drained down his throat. He belched without covering his mouth.

"Help yourself," she said sarcastically.

He raised the empty can saying, "Thanks. Don't mind if I do." He grabbed another can and popped the top.

"So, what's my read on David Levy?" she echoed. "In what way?"

He took a long swig of beer, muffled a burp and wiped his lips. "Just generally speaking."

"Well, he's definitely not in my Brad Pitt look-alike contest. That yucky coffee screwed up his chances of becoming a movie star."

"Get serious," he demanded.

"Duh," she jibed. "I'll get serious if you'll be more specific."

Cassidy's wrinkled brow showed unaccustomed mental exercise. "Is Levy an honest person?"

"Gee. Let me think about that one. An honest hedge fund manager. Wow, talk about an oxymoron. Terry, why don't you get to the point? Someplace behind that empty stare a thought stirs."

He stiffened proudly. "Try this one on for size. David Levy will be arrested on Monday morning."

"Arrested for what and by whom?"

"Embezzling. Levy will, in my opinion, go down as one of the biggest white-collar criminals in the history of Wall Street."

"Hold on a second. Who's arresting Levy?"

"The district attorney."

She looked incredulous. "Good luck proving anything. Levy's no dummy. And if he is guilty, he's probably already hauled ass to a country without extradition."

Atkinson sneered. "He's been under surveillance around-the-clock."

"If you're telling me Levy opened new accounts to pay old accounts' fictitious returns and that he skimmed millions off the top, I'm not buying it. He wasn't running a Ponzi scheme."

"Levy isn't your run-of-the-mill crook. He's far more ingenious."

"You mean ingenious as in Machiavellian?" she asked.

Cassidy manufactured an intelligent expression, but his eyes revealed incomprehension. He went on offense to save face. "I'm gonna make this as simple as I can."

She continued to smirk. "Okay, Mister Steven Hawking. Hey, I didn't fail the New York bar exam umpteen times."

"Thanks, I needed that." After retrieving the last can of Heinekens, he began to build his case. "Let's say we both manage hedge funds.

To the world at large, Jackie Atkinson and Terry Cassidy are complete strangers who just happened to manage hedge funds. The kicker is we're secretly in cahoots." He slurped some beer and suppressed another belch. "For the sake of argument, let's say our hedge funds both have one billion dollars in assets. Let's call your fund the Cain fund. And mine the Abel fund. Remember, our investors don't know we're in business together. I work in London. You work here in New York. Hedge funds charge a two-percent management fee plus twenty percent of the profits. And more importantly, they don't participate in the clients' losses. That means we both make two million dollars in annual upfront fees."

She blew a strand of hair out of her eyes. "No wonder you flunked the bar. Two percent equals twenty million each."

"I needed to make sure you were paying attention."

Jackie crossed her legs and then re-crossed them. "Yeah, right."

"Okay, let's assume you're bullish and you're right on the market. You leverage your Cain fund to the hilt on the buy side. I do the exact opposite with my Abel fund by shorting the market. The market takes off and you make forty percent for your investors. Conversely, I lose forty percent for my investors. We secretly split the forty percent of your investors' four hundred million in profits. Which amounts to...?" He started to pour beer into her glass, but having second thoughts drained the can.

"On the sly we split two hundred million. Not a bad day's pay," she answered and added, "I guess math wasn't required at Kentucky or wherever you played basketball. I find that rather unusual for an accounting major."

He ignored her taunt and continued, "Here's the real kicker. Since I don't participate in the profits until my investors get all of their money back, I say I'm sorry things didn't work out and I closeout their accounts. Assuming we can reload with more gullible investors, its déjà vu."

"It's like hiring Bonnie and Clyde to guard Fort Knox," she said in a voice tainted by a poorly imitated southern twang.

"Damn straight. Word gets out you were up forty percent we'd have drooling investors standing in line with their checkbooks."

She looked skeptical again "But can you prove David Levy broke the law?"

"Not only can I prove it, I have evidence showing he siphoned off profitable trades into the accounts of people in very high places."

She looked surprised. "I thought the old guided trading scam ended after that ex-president's wife made a hundred grand trading cattle futures."

"Old swindles never die, they just mutate." He explained that Levy's real moneymaker was running hedge funds with opposing investment philosophies in four different countries. Raking in twenty percent of the profits made Levy filthy rich, and the losses, well, that was someone else's problem. Cassidy stated that charities, foundations, even pension accounts were the victims.

"Terry, I *do* believe you've found your calling. You're a whistleblower."

He confessed that he never intended to pursue a career with the SEC. After receiving a tip from one of Levy's disgruntled ex-employees, Cassidy approached the district attorney with the idea of worming his way into the SEC to gather evidence against Levy. He confided that initially, the DA's office didn't approve of his plan, but now they were more than willing to reap the rewards from putting a titan of Wall Street behind bars.

She hesitated for a spell staring at him expectantly. "What's this got to do with you saving my ass?"

"C'mon, Jackie, you can't be serious. You know how Bernie Madoff affected the SEC. Lots of red faces and shortened careers. When the shit hits the fan, you can bet the commissioner will be looking for a sacrificial lamb. Take it to the bank."

"But why me?" she asked defensively.

"He's not above saying you overlooked certain accounting irregularities at Global because you were having an affair with a man hired by Levy to... You finish the sentence. Get the picture?"

"How dare you...?" she hissed. Her eyes came to life as she unruffled her blouse. Her look was more from embarrassment than indignation. Pink cheeks reappeared.

"God damn it, Jackie, we wiretapped Levy's telephone. It ain't pretty."

She sighed despondently. Finally, she said, "How could I have been so stupid?" Her mind drifted back to the times she'd discussed her work at Global with Andre. She even caught him reading her confidential memos. "He played me like a fiddle."

"Don't blame yourself."

"I don't deserve this. Don't say what you're thinking, Terry. And by the way, part of this is your fault."

"My fault?" he asked.

"After we...you know. You acted like nothing happened."

Cassidy narrowed one eye. "Look, I didn't dump you, you dumped me. Just for the record, I majored in criminal justice, not accounting."

"You and every college athlete in America," she jeered. "I'm screwed, and there's nothing I can do about it." And not by that good-for-nothing Andre, she thought. "Levy ruined my life, what there is of it."

He ignored her slight saying, "Not necessarily. There is a way to save your butt." Cassidy recited what he called his cover-your-ass letter. He advised her to send the following text to her supervisor:

Dear Sir:

I have genuine concerns about David Levy's company, Global Investments. Although Global passed the annual audit by the guidelines set forth by the commission, I feel a more comprehensive review is warranted. I would welcome the opportunity to discuss my misgivings with you at your earliest convenience.

Jacqueline Atkinson

Senior Auditor

She laced her hands behind her head and looked up him. "Why are you helping me?"

"That's not hard to figure." His eyes answered her question.

"I owe you one," she said, standing up. She kissed him softly on the cheek.

"You don't owe me a thing," he said returning her kiss.

"Terry, what's your sign?"

"I'm a Sagittarius. We don't believe in Astronomy."

Instead of mocking him, she kissed him deeply. He parodied her acquired southern drawl. "Ah, shucks ma'am, it weren't nothing. Is there anything else I can do for you?"

She batted her eyes seductively and blushed secretly. "Well, now that you mention it."

Terry spoke with a silly grin painted on his face. "Wouldn't this be considered sexual harassment? I mean technically, you are my boss."

"Terry, you already resigned. Now, turn off the lights."

"Are you gonna vote for me when I run for mayor."

"Only if you stop talking."

James Gardner

8

David Levy sat alone on the landscaped balcony of his penthouse apartment overlooking Central Park. He'd hosted a weekend party at his sprawling Long Island estate in East Hampton. His guest list included the usual assortment of always-available society tramps and married stockbrokers on-the-make with a few aspiring movie stars and politicians thrown into the mix. Normally, a weekend of cocaine and booze would leave him exhausted, but his meeting with the SEC auditors had unnerved him enough to keep him straight. The fear of going to prison was never far from his thoughts. As a precaution, he'd put the first stage of his disappearing strategy in motion. He washed down an Ambien with a sip of Remy Martin and decided to call it a night.

At 3:30, Levy's telephone rang. After his heart rate slowed, he checked the caller ID. The call was originating from Washington, D.C. No one in his right mind asks for a political donation at this hour, he realized picking up the receiver.

"Is this David Levy?" the caller inquired.

"Do you know what time it is?"

"Are you the David Levy who runs Global Investments?"

Levy's heart skipped a beat "Yes, that's right. Who's calling?"

The caller's tone of voice sounded unrepentant, almost giddy. "Sorry about calling you so late, Mr. Levy. We thought you'd like to know, you're gonna be arrested in your office tomorrow morning at ten o'clock."

"Arrested for what and by whom?"

"Our advice, hire the best lawyers you can find or... Fill in the blanks, Mr. Levy."

"Do you have any idea how much money I've given you fucking morons?"

"Pleasant dreams, Mr. Levy."

"Who is this?" Levy demanded again. The anonymous caller hung up. He listened to the dial tone for a few long moments and then he hung up.

Levy jumped out of bed and ran to the bathroom. As he stood under an ice-cold shower his mind fast-forwarded. The years of rehearsing were about to be put to the test. The plan had always been to leave at a moment's notice. There could be no attachments, nothing to slow him down. After a quick line of cocaine to counteract the sleeping pill, Levy slipped into a jogging suit and sneakers.

He retrieved a Smith and Wesson 9mm from a wall safe hidden behind a watercolor.

God, I hate leaving this, Levy thought admiring the Homer Winslow. He shoveled four counterfeit passports, packets of five different currencies and a cigar box of perfect ten-carat diamonds into a Hermes briefcase.

The last item was a large manila envelope containing a list of political donations and the photo-static copies of illegally guided commodity transactions. He hoped the incriminating evidence would insure a presidential pardon. It was his ace in the hole.

As he ran to the service elevator, he checked his watch; it was four o'clock. *A six o'clock takeoff gives me a four-hour head start.* The doorman didn't see him slip out a backdoor connected to the underground garage. Levy glanced at his Phantom Rolls Royce and the Bugatti Vitese. The thought of losing his cars was nauseating, but making a clean getaway meant leaving everything, he reminded himself again. The die was cast. There was no turning back.

Levy ran across Fifth Avenue and entered Central Park near the zoo. It was a moonless night. He pinched his collar together. The sounds of the city were muffled by the trees. After walking a short distance he thought he heard footsteps and heavy breathing. Someone was following him. Levy slipped behind a tree, drew and cocked his pistol. Only the fear of being revealed stopped him from firing. It was an insomniac runner jogging in the same direction. He exhaled a long breath and continued walking. There were no more encounters. He exiting the Park at 59th Street and hailed a taxicab.

As the taxi entered the Lincoln Tunnel, the cabdriver tried to engage Levy in conversation. "How about our idiot mayor trying to eighty-six the horse carriages—can you believe this creep? Guy's a jerk-off. Know what I mean?" The last thing Levy wanted was to be remembered by a cabby. *Most taxi-drivers don't speak English and I get mister big-mouth,* he thought. He ignored the driver and checked his messages. A text from his chief pilot confirmed his Falcon-2000 was fueled and standing by. The pilot asked him for a final destination to facilitate a flight plan. Levy emailed the pilot back telling him that he could file a flight plan after they were airborne. The plan had always been to disappear into Africa.

How he got there was another matter. He planned to make his disappearance as difficult as possible for his pursuers.

9

Monday afternoon
FBI Regional office
Manhattan

The unsuccessful arrest of David Levy was a comedy of errors. To make a bad situation worse, a television crew had been called in to record the arrest. The attempt to improve the reputation of the FBI had backfired. There were lots of red faces.

The FBI's Deputy Director, Allan Greenberg, sat at one end of an oval conference table. The United States attorney for the southern district of New York occupied the other end. Next to him, the SEC's deputy director conversed quietly with New York's district attorney and his two female assistants. James Middleton, a lawyer representing the National Security Agency, sat next to Greenberg. Terrance Cassidy and Jacqueline Atkinson were relegated to back row seats along the wall. The atmosphere in the room was very tense. Allen Greenberg's bitter frown was repeated by everyone at the table. Greenberg looked up from the subpoena papers and swept his audience with a seething glance. "This hasn't exactly been a blue-ribbon day for me. Anyone care to comment?" The ensuing silence was deafening. He looked directly at the district attorney and announced, "Sir, you assured me that..." He referred to his notes.

"That every precaution was being implemented to insure the uneventful arrest of David Levy. Are those your words?" If looks could kill, the DA would have died on the spot.

"Yes, but..." answered the DA.

Greenberg interrupted him. "As we both know, that's not what happened. I let you stage a media event and look what happened. You orchestrated a colossal goat-fuck. And now I look like an incompetent fool."

The DA nodded dejectedly saying, "Our records indicate that David Levy received a telephone call from Washington six hours prior to the failed attempt to take him into custody."

"Inferring what, that we have leaks in our government? I've got news for you. Leaks are endemic in Washington. They always have been and they always will be. At this point, playing the blame-game is total bullshit," Greenberg said, avoiding his own condemnation.

The DA made another stab at diverting responsibility. "I'm just saying..."

Greenberg cut him off again. "And where does this leave us?" The room went silent. "It would seem to me that the only individuals in this room, and I include myself, who know what the hell's going on are Miss Atkinson and Mr. Cassidy." All eyes were drawn to Jackie and Terry. Their expressions remained stoic. When the group looked away, Atkinson nudged Cassidy in the ribs.

Greenberg produced a photograph of David Levy from a folder and studied it thoughtfully. "Mr. Levy's apprehension is crucial to two very high-profile candidates in Washington, who, for obvious reasons, shall remain anonymous. There are circumstances surrounding this case I'm not at liberty to discuss, at least not yet. Greenberg scanned the participants. "Come on, gentlemen. I need input. Let's start with David Levy's background."

The DA's senior assistant gained the floor by standing up. She told them that David Levy was born and raised in Brooklyn. He was an exceptional student, receiving scholarships from Exeter Academy, Yale and, later, Harvard Law School. He was married briefly to an Israeli citizen. He was divorced and had no children and no living relatives. His net worth was estimated to be north of five-hundred million dollars. He was a major contributor to both the current administration as well as the leading democratic candidate in the upcoming presidential election. Upon hearing Levy's political affiliation, Greenberg's bushy eyebrows drew tighter. "Anyone care to speculate as to our suspect's whereabouts? For all we know, he might be anywhere."

The DA's other female assistant spoke up. "Sir, Levy's private aircraft departed U.S. airspace at 0900 hours. The international flight plan listed Sao Paulo, Brazil, as the final destination. We've alerted the Brazilian police."

"And?" Greenberg asked raising his voice.

"At this point, they're not cooperating. Apparently, greasing palms works wonders in Brazil."

"So, reading between the lines, you're telling me that Levy will seek asylum someplace in South America?"

Before the woman could answer, Jackie Atkinson piped up from the back of the room. "Sir, Levy won't stay in South America."

"Miss Atkinson, if you have something to add to these proceedings, please do so," insisted Greenberg.

Reluctantly, Atkinson stood up. "Levy will wind up in Israel."

"And what makes you say that, Miss Atkinson?"

"Because he never stopped talking about Israel. How beautiful it was and how he planned to retire there. Israel was the only place in the world he truly felt safe."

"Excellent. What else have you got for us?" Greenberg asked.

Atkinson said that the first time she met David Levy, he insisted on taking her to lunch. After a bottle of wine, he became chatty. He seemed disillusioned about great wealth's making people happy. He acted depressed and at times, distracted. According to him, life was meaningless. When he spoke about Israel, his behavior improved.

Greenberg sat motionless, unblinking as Atkinson spoke. When she stopped, he sighed. "Anyone care to add anything?"

When Cassidy raised his hand and stood up, Atkinson thought, please don't say anything stupid. Cassidy asked, "Sir, can I look at Levy's photograph?" Greenberg handed the picture to the man sitting next to him who passed it back to Cassidy. Cassidy studied Levy's portrait for a few seconds before handing it to Jackie. "It's not Levy," Cassidy announced.

"What? You can't be serious?" Greenberg barked in a rumbling baritone voice. He banged his clinched fist on the table to emphasis his displeasure. "Let me get this straight. You're telling me this isn't David Levy."

"It's not him, or at least this photograph doesn't look anything like Levy." Cassidy explained that the private offices of Wall Street bigwigs were usually adorned with photographs of themselves posing with famous professional athletes or shaking hand with politicians or standing next to celebrities. Levy displayed no such photographs. The pictures in Levy's office were of his expensive toys. He concluded by saying that Levy had undergone extensive plastic surgery and as such, his appearance had been altered.

Greenberg rubbed the fatigue from his eyes. "Talk about a nightmare. So, what's your conclusion, Mr. Cassidy? If I might be so bold to ask."

"That you won't find any current photographs of David Levy, because he's been planning his disappearing act for a long time."

"Miss Atkinson thinks Levy will make his way to Israel. Do you concur?" Greenberg asked Cassidy.

"It might be a diversion. At this point, it's hard to tell fact from fiction with this guy." Cassidy nodded at Atkinson, she gave him an affirmative nod in return.

Greenberg pounded the table again. "So, Levy isn't your average Wall Street maggot. He's an intelligent, well-connected, well-financed thief on the lam. And if Mr. Cassidy's right about his planning this for a long time, he'll be traveling on a false passport. Does that pretty well sum it up?"

The gloomy nods indicated that everyone agreed. Greenberg eyed the DA with contempt. He snagged the man's elbow. "Sir, I'd like to borrow Mr. Cassidy, if that's all right with you. He looked at the man representing the SEC and asked, "Think you can spare Miss Atkinson?"

"For as long as you need her." The DA acquiesced hoping Greenberg wouldn't go public pointing fingers. "The same goes for Mr. Cassidy."

"At least they can identify Levy. If we move fast, we just might catch our man before he disappears. Greenberg glanced at Atkinson, then Cassidy and asked with new life in his voice, "Are you both in agreement with my appraisal of the situation?"

Jackie said, "We're good with it." They both nodded.

"Absolutely," Cassidy added.

"Good. Then, it's a go." Greenberg whispered to his assistant who got up from the table and left the room. When the assistant returned he had two men in tow who were introduced as FBI agents. "Miss Atkinson, Mr. Cassidy, these men will accompany you to Brazil, forthwith. Let's hope our fugitive hasn't had enough time to depart South America. One more thing—your diplomacy is vitally important in this matter. Are we all on the same page?" After seeing their favorable responses, Greenberg added, "I'm counting on you two."

As Cassidy and Jackie walked out of the room, Jackie whispered, "I was afraid you might make an ass of yourself in there."

Cassidy grinned. "Oh, ye of little faith."

Jackie grabbed his hand. "Terry, sometimes you surprise me. You really do."

"So, does that mean you wanna have my children?"

"You've got a one-track mind."

"Speaking of asses, yours is world-class.

Jackie shook her head.

10

Sáo Paulo

David Levy's pilots were shocked when Levy handed them a manila envelope containing $25,000. There were two strings attached. He wanted them to remain in Rio de Janeiro for two weeks. Secondly, if the police questioned them about Levy's whereabouts, they agreed not to cooperate. As Levy explained, he was the subject of a politically motivated investigation. He needed two weeks to clear his name.

As a precaution, Levy told the pilots that he was staying at the Hotel de Casco in Buenos Aires. Instead of traveling south to Argentina, he worked his way north to Caracas, Venezuela. His misgivings about the pilots were well-founded. Two days later, the drunken pilots were arrested in one of Rio's infamous brothels. After spending two hellish nights in jail, they traded information about Levy in exchange for their immediate release. The deception had worked.

Fearing security cameras and metal detectors, Levy avoided airports and upscale hotels. He traveled on native buses, bought food from street vendors and slept in flop houses. In spite of the fortune David Levy had in his possession, he blended into the underbelly of South America as an ordinary tourist.

One week after landing at the Sao Paulo Airport, he booked passage on the Venezuelan oil tanker, Amazonian.

The transatlantic voyage from Caracas to Durban, South Africa, would take two weeks. David Levy had successfully covered his tracks.

As Levy watched the Venezuelan coastline slip beneath the Amazonian's boiling wake, he considered his future. As instructed, his Washington lawyers continued to pursue a reduction of the charges against him and the possibility of a presidential pardon. Levy had given millions to the current administration, but outgoing politicians are notorious backstabbers. His hope for a no-questions-asked exoneration had stalled. The upcoming presidential election would tip the scales in his favor. For now, his best option was to disappear.

David Levy spent the next two weeks locked in his stateroom. His cocaine addiction fueled delusional fantasies. He became convinced that members of the Amazonian's crew were conspiring to rob him. Sleep became so illusive; Levy lost twenty pounds during the Atlantic crossing. He disembarked in Durban, South Africa, as an emaciated shadow of himself. His disguise was even more complete. Levy's self-deception excluded one reality; he knew the list of people who wanted him silenced was long and growing.

11

Six months later
New York City

It had been six months since David Levy's disappearance. From time to time he was reportedly seen in Africa, but gradually the news about him subsided. When a video of Levy's beheading appeared on the internet everything changed. The same administration that turned down his request for a presidential pardon was apoplectic about his execution. One high-profile politician was very relieved. The link between her and David Levy had been severed or so it seemed.

Terrance Cassidy may have lacked above-average mental acuity, but he had street-smarts in spades. He'd launched his law career on David Levy's arrest and prosecution. Now he was just another assistant district attorney mired in run-of-the-mill cases. He needed something to revitalize his standing with the district attorney. That's when Cassidy decided to reincarnate David Levy. On a hunch, he transmitted an anonymous email to one of London's leading newspaper reporters. Out of the blue, Levy sightings started appearing on the internet. The last one occurred at a hotel in Mombasa. If David Levy was alive, who was the man executed?

Cassidy's unsigned email was forwarded to the London's foreign correspondent in New York City.

Within hours that text was forwarded to the heads of DNC and the RNC in Washington. Any connection to Levy was political suicide. Levy's large political donations should have been returned because they were derived from ill-gotten gains, but that wasn't in the cards. The money was squirreled away in politicians' war-chests. It didn't take long for the Levy problem to reach a lawyer representing the leading presidential candidate who turned to his longtime friend and confident, the chief legal counsel for the National Security Agency, James Middleton. After the usual political gossip, the DNC lawyer said, "Jim, we've been friends a long time. This conversation is off the record. Agreed?"

"Yes, of course."

"The David Levy problem won't go away. I'm being pressured."

"Pressured by whom? The man is dead."

"You know he's dead and I know he's dead. But unnamed politicians are shitting in their pants."

"You're telling me they're worried about the internet bullshit?"

"It's more complicated than that. Levy's lawyers are saying he kept a detailed record of his political donations. We're talking about tens of millions. There are people willing to do anything to get their hands on that list."

"Hey, shouldn't we stay clear of this?" Middleton knew the answer, but he wanted his friend's response on the record.

"Jim, please don't play the innocent card with me. It's beneath you. I'm coming to you as a friend, God damn it."

"Look, I'm just saying..."

"Spare me the cover-your-ass minutiae. Sometimes what we do is ethically indefensible and incredibly necessary. It ain't pretty, but it's the way of the world, my friend."

Middleton had to be careful. There was a thin line between who played whom. "Hope this doesn't come back to bite us in the ass, that's all I'm saying."

The lawyer cut in. "Levy contributed a fortune to her campaign fund and their foundation. To hedge his bet, he gave to the other candidate. They won't return the money unless they're ordered to do so by a court. Money's tight and so are the poll numbers. This isn't chump change we're talking about. Everyone wants this thing put to bed."

"Why all the interest now?"

"It started with that fucking email."

"Can't computer forensics identify the sender?" Middleton asked.

"The email in question was traced to a computer in the offices of New York's district attorney. Hundreds have access."

Middleton spoke more for himself saying, "Why would the DA...unless?"

"It's not the DA. Of that, I'm certain. Unless what? What're you thinking?"

Middleton hesitated as a mental picture formulated. "I know who might be responsible. There's a new lackey in the DA's office. Guy's a shameless self-promoter. He's the one who fingered Levy in the first place."

"Say you're right. How do we find out whose pulling his strings?" the lawyer asked. "We've got three months to the election. After that, Levy will be a footnote in criminal law books."

"What would you suggest?" Middleton asked.

"Okay, Levy was killed on his yacht. The yacht has been impounded in Africa. Levy's black book is on that yacht, I'd bet my life on it. Send the emailing son-of-a-bitch to Africa. At least that'll give us some breathing room."

Middleton asked, "Will the DA play ball? In other words, can we trust him?"

"I would have to say, yes."

Middleton hesitated. "What if...?"

"What were you gonna say?"

"What if David Levy isn't dead?"

"He's deader than Elvis. You know it and I know it. Hell, the world knows it."

Middleton said, "Not granting Levy a presidential pardon was a huge mistake. If the right people had petitioned him, the president would've rubber-stamped it."

"It's a little late for that now. What's done is done," said the lawyer.

Middleton thumbed through his rolodex until he came to the letter C. "I'm on it."

"Jim, I assure you, your loyalty won't be unnoticed."

Middleton knew the carrot routine by heart. He mouthed his friend's response internally. "Someday, you'll need our help. We'll be there for you. It doesn't hurt to be in good standing with the incoming administration. Next time you're in Washington, let's tee it up at Congressional. Say hello to your wife for me. And thanks, Jimmy, I knew I could count on you."

"Glad I could help." Middleton closed his eyes. His mind drifted to thoughts of an early retirement.

James Middleton's lunch invitation intrigued Cassidy. He guessed his plan to reinvent David Levy had worked. Where that might lead him was a mystery. They met at the Oyster Bar above Grand Central Station. The dining room smelled like clams and Clorox. Cassidy was waiting at the bar when Middleton arrived. They shook hands. "Nice to see you again, Mr. Cassidy. How are things at the DA's office?"

Cassidy loosened his tie like it was a hangman's noose. "Hectic."

They chitchatted over bowls of fish chowder.

Eventually, they ran out of things to say. "Sir, I'm due in court. You wanted to see me because...?" Cassidy asked.

"Mr. Cassidy, I like candor. Ever think about a career with the National Security Agency?"

"I'm sure your standards are too high for me. I graduated at the bottom of my class."

Middleton spoke as if he hadn't heard Cassidy. "Let me know if you ever change your mind. Off the record, I'd like your opinion about a sensitive situation."

"Shoot."

"Is David Levy dead or alive?"

Cassidy shot him an empty stare; it was his trademark expression. "The photograph on the internet certainly says he's dead."

Middleton whispered out of the corner of his mouth, "But are you positive the man in the photograph was Levy?"

"Sir, I can't say for sure."

"Why not?"

"Because, like I testified, his face was too…, you get the picture." Cassidy cringed inwardly as the image flashed before his mind's eye.

Middleton's expression remained passive. "Levy's reincarnation is making some people in Washington very nervous. I'm speaking about the press's fascination with the internet idiocy."

"So, you're telling me you believe Levy is alive." Even though Cassidy started the rumor, he couldn't help remember how Jackie said the execution seemed too orchestrated—like an overused plot in a B movie.

Middleton said, "I didn't say David Levy was alive. In fact, I'm positive the opposite is true. It's just that out of the blue, he's seen at some fancy resort in Africa. Its internet drivel, but the press loves this stuff."

Cassidy's pulse elevated. "What's this gotta do with me?"

"I'll get to that in a minute. Our computer experts are tracing the original email as we speak. Middleton's claim made Cassidy squirm. Cassidy tried to act blasé, but his eyes revealed total panic.

I was right, it was you, Middleton thought.

Middleton looked squarely into Cassidy's eyes. "Why would someone send an anonymous email to a London newspaper to resurrect the David Levy saga? It's hard to figure."

Cassidy shook his head.

"Anyway, I thought about you and your connection to Levy."

Cassidy looked frightened. "Sorry, you lost me."

Middleton enjoyed torturing Cassidy. "I meant you can identify David Levy." Middleton's partial truth would go unchallenged.

"But you just said you believe Levy was in fact, executed."

Middleton said, "Look, let's be honest with each other. I'm betting the Levy screw-up damaged your standing with the DA. As they say, success has a million fathers and failure is an orphan."

"I'm lower than snake shit with the DA."

"Do this favor for me and I'll make sure you're rewarded. And if I've sent you on a wild goose chase, that is to say, you find evidence that Levy was in fact executed, better yet." When Cassidy appeared shocked, Middleton tempered his words. "Look, I didn't mean it that way. It's just that investors lost their life's savings with Levy. Hard to feel sympathy for the man."

Cassidy appeared confused. "Favor? What kind of a favor?"

"I'd like you to go to Kenya for me. Be my eyes and ears, so to speak."

Cassidy's brow furrowed.

Middleton continued, "We know Levy kept a book or a ledger or a computer run of his foreign bank accounts. I believe that list is still onboard his yacht. As we both know, his yacht has been quarantined in Kenya."

"Kenya is a long way from here," Cassidy mentioned.

"You *do* know the trustee is offering a percentage of the any funds recovered? We're talking about what could be seven figures. As they say, 'follow the money' and the trail starts in Kenya."

The talk of money piqued Cassidy's interest. He emitted a low whistle. "I need to speak to my boss."

"I've already cleared this with the DA. These are your airline tickets to Nairobi, expense money, a credit card and everything you ever wanted to know about David Levy. The Kenyan police will meet you at the airport." Middleton handed him a thick manila envelope. "Do this for me and I'll find a place for you in Washington. You've got my word on it."

"My girlfriend's gonna raise hell."

"Oh, I'm sure she can spare you for a few days. One more thing, all communications should be with me and me only. My private number is in there," he said handing Cassidy an untraceable cell phone. Have a safe trip. Almost wish I was going with you."

Jackie Atkinson's commuter flight from Washington to La Guardia landed on time. She'd been waiting at O'Neal's Wake for almost an hour when Cassidy burst through the front door. What he whispered to a barmaid made the woman blush.

"The usual, TC?" yelled the bartender in a voice deepened by thirty years of cigarette smoke.

"Yup, beer and a double bump," Cassidy shouted back.

Jackie embraced Cassidy with a peck on his cheek.

"So, how was your day?" she asked him as they sat down in a booth. He looks like the cat that just swallowed a canary, she thought.

"Couldn't have been better. Get this—I'm going on a paid vacation to Kenya. How do you like them apples?"

Jackie hiked her perfectly tweezed eyebrows. "And that's good, because...?"

"Hey, I was going nowhere. A big-time lawyer with the National Security Agency thinks this could be my career-changer."

"You're going to Africa? Sorry, I don't see the connection."

Cassidy briefed her on his efforts to reinvigorate the David Levy saga. He reminded her that she was the one who raised concerns about the authenticity of his execution. "When in doubt, always blame the radical Muslims," she said. And he remembered her saying that Levy seemed too intelligent to get himself kidnapped. Now, he was being sent to Africa to investigate David Levy's execution. The sweetener was the reward money offered by the trustee.

As Jackie half-listened, she imagined what it would be like to be married to Terrance Cassidy. He's got major faults, but I can change him. Our kids won't be rocket scientists, but they will be beautiful.

After he stopped speaking, a mental alarm went off. "Terry, what computer did you use to send that email?"

"One in the office. And yes, I deleted it," he replied with a self-assured smirk locked on his face.

Poor thing doesn't know you can never totally delete emails. Jackie decided not to raise the issue. She had a more pressing matter.

He grinned around an unlit cigar and put his arm around her shoulders. "How about some wine, sweetheart?"

"I quit."

"You quit? When did this happen?"

Jackie glanced at her Rolex. "About five hours ago."

"How come?"

She put her hand on top of his. "Terry, I'm pregnant."

His cigar hit the floor

12

Nairobi

Terrance Cassidy's African experience got off to an inauspicious beginning. He disembarked the British Airlines flight in Nairobi wearing a designer Abercrombie safari outfit that included a khaki hunting jacket trimmed with bullet loops, leather boots and an Indiana-Jones style hat wrapped in a zebra skin hatband. He would have attracted less attention if he'd deplaned wearing a thong.

As Cassidy waited in the Kenyan Customs and Immigration queue, he was approached by a young black man who told him he could expedite his entry into Kenya for a small fee. He took Cassidy's passport and disappeared. Thirty minutes later, Cassidy was told by a second man that it would cost him $500 to get his passport back. Reluctantly, he paid the man.

The police escorts assigned to meet Cassidy arrived one-hour late, which was considered punctual by African standards. "*Jambo*, Mr. Cassidy," said the off-duty policeman.

His partner questioned Cassidy. "Why haven't you cleared Kenyan Customs?" Cassidy described the perpetrators who scammed him. Within minutes, they returned with his passport and the $500. One policeman said to the other in Swahili, "I thought you said Americans were intelligent people."

His partner shrugged and warned Cassidy, "One must be very cautious while traveling in Africa. There are many, many criminals roaming about."

The policemen forced back grins.

"Can I ask you two a question?" Cassidy inquired as he climbed into the backseat of their unmarked Toyota Land Cruiser. "Are there any al-Qaeda jihadists around here?"

"Do you mean at this airport or in Kenya?"

"Jesus Christ! Let's start with Kenya."

"Too many to count," confessed the policeman. "Don't worry. You are now under police protection."

"Well, that's a fucking relief. I understand we're taking the train to Mombasa?"

"The train to Mombasa is temporarily not operating due to repairs."

"How long will it be out of service," Cassidy asked.

The policeman looked at his colleague saying, "The train to Mombasa stopped running two years ago."

Jetlag was beginning to take a toll on Cassidy. He squeezed the bridge of his nose. "You guys must work for the Chamber of Commerce. So, what's our alternative?"

Neither policeman fathomed his cynicism. "We are chauffeuring you to Mombasa, sir." Cassidy was afraid to hear the specifics, but he asked anyway, "How long will that take?"

"It depends on the condition of the roads. But first, we must deliver you to your hotel."

Cassidy leaned against the front seat. "What's the name of my hotel again?"

The policeman beamed saying, "The Norfolk is Nairobi's finest hotel."

"Hey, wasn't the Norfolk bombed in a terrorist attack?"

"Yes, but many years ago."

"How can it get any worse?" Cassidy muttered rhetorically.

The policemen glanced at each other. One man remarked to his partner in Swahili, "The mzungu is a pain in my ass. If I were al-Qaeda, I would kill him myself." His partner nodded vigorously saying, "He talks more than your wife."

"No one talks more than my wife."

The 275-mile drive from Nairobi to Mombasa should have taken a day. The policemen had been ordered to stall Cassidy. They faked two mechanical breakdowns. There wasn't a need to fabricate the three tire punctures. The roundabout journey took three days.

As soon as they arrived in Mombasa, Cassidy insisted they drive him to the city's waterfront district. After questioning the captains of five fishing boats, Cassidy sought out the port harbormaster who said he'd seen David Levy's yacht, the Black Cygnet, three months ago. The yacht had set sail for Dar es Salaam, Tanzania or ports further south.

Cassidy didn't know he'd been sent on a fool's errand. Come hell or high water, Cassidy was determined to find out what happened to David Levy.

Clearing Tanzanian customs was uneventful. He hired a driver for the trip to the city's seaport. Tanzania's largest port was a beehive of activity. Ships from all corners of the world lay at anchor. Other ships moored against wharfs loaded and unloaded cargo containers. Giant derricks stacked the containers on the docks like building blocks. Tugboats belched black smoke as they pushed and towed freighters and oil tankers. An armada of smaller vessels scurried between the anchored ships. Screeching seagulls fought over floating garbage.

The port manager's office was located in the Ministry of Transport building. The sign on the door read: HARBOUR PILOT BACK IN FIFTEEN MINUTES

Cassidy scanned a shipping schedule as he waited on a bench under a shady banyan tree. One hour later, he followed the bearded harbormaster into his office. He was light-complexioned and looked more Arab than African. He wore a plaid threadbare sport coat and a tie. The color combination indicated possible colorblindness. The coat was a few sizes too large. "What can I do for you?" he asked with snotty annoyance.

"I'm looking for this boat." He handed the harbormaster a photograph of the Black Cygnet."

"But this isn't a boat. It's a sailing vessel, sir."

"Whatever it is, I need to find it."

The harbormaster shook his head. "I have no knowledge of this, this... vessel." The man reeked of starched arrogance.

"You're sure about that? Maybe a Benjamin Franklin will improve your memory." Cassidy laid a one hundred-dollar bill on the man's desk. The harbormaster's attitude improved.

He snatched the hundred off of the desk with the speed of a striking viper and secured the money in his breast pocket. "Give me the vessel's name again?" He picked up the telephone and stared at Cassidy as he conversed in Swahili. When he was finished speaking he patted the desk indicating he wanted more. Cassidy gave him another hundred. "What do you want with this vessel, sir?" he asked reexamining the photograph.

"So, you do know something?" Cassidy asked evading his question. He could hardly contain himself.

"My contact says the Black Cygnet is currently in route from Zanzibar. She will be moored at a shipyard here for repairs in two days." He scribbled the address on a scrap of a paper and handed it to Cassidy. "What's your business in Tanzania?"   Cassidy walked out the office without answering.

13

Zimbabwe

As Rigby drove to the Victoria Falls Airport, he told Lily about Otto Bern. Otto started his aviation career flying Hawker Hunters for the Rhodesian Air Force. He had flown in almost every country on the African continent. He didn't tell her that Otto had done time in prison for arms smuggling. Nor did he tell her that Otto was missing a few body parts. Thanks to a landmine, Otto was missing a leg from the knee down. A nasty bite from a puff adder had cost him three fingers. An ear had been amputated in an airplane crash. The natives said that Africa was whittling on Otto like termites eating a mopani stump.

They found Otto with his head buried under the engine cowl of his vintage Piper Cherokee. He whistled a tune, but a lack of dentures and no musical proclivities made the effort sound like air escaping from a punctured tire.

"Well, if it ain't the old African jailbird. Croxford, make yourself useful, hand me that adjustable spanner," Otto yelled in English polluted by Afrikaans. His face was covered with so much grease he looked like a blackface performer in a Vaudeville production. His watery eyes bulged a little, giving him a permanent expression of indignation. When he saw Lily, he discreetly replaced his dentures. The false teeth were as white as piano keys and looked out of place in such a weathered face.

"Lily Rosen, this is Otto Bern or what's left of him." Lily tried unsuccessfully to shake Otto's better hand. His fingernails were black deep into the quicks.

"My dear, I'm charmed." Otto showed her his greasy palm before wiping it on his sweat-stained overalls.

Lily said, "I've heard a lot about you. Rigby says you're the best pilot in Africa.

"I must tell you, Croxford is a known exaggerator. Did he tell you about the time we crash-landed in the Sudan?"

"Not yet." Lily replied.

"It was quite thrilling, to say the least."

"Otto, you're the only pilot in the world that could have made that landing, not to mention the takeoff. The best part, we walked away without a scratch. I'd crash with you anytime."

Otto's prosthesis made it difficult for him to climb down from the scaffolding surrounding the Piper's fuselage. He muttered a few choice curse words under his breath.

"Croxford, something tells me this isn't a social visit." He pivoted on his good leg and addressed Lily. "What can I do for you, young lady?"

"I want to rent your airplane."

Otto started to speak, but his dislodged false teeth prevented him. He realigned them with his tongue and asked, "Charter my plane for what purpose?"

"Fly us to Mozambique and then north along the coastline."

"How far north?" Otto half-rolled his eyes.

"All the way to Cairo, if need be."

"I must say, it does sound rather enticing. No need to give me the particulars. Croxford, I know if you're involved in this, it must be something dodgy, which is right up my alley. So, what's our timeframe? In other words, when do we leave?"

"How about tomorrow morning," Lily answered, looking at Rigby for confirmation.

Otto looked disappointed. "Bugger all. My bird's got a busted wing. Cracked a piston taking off from an island in the Okavango Swamp. It'll take me a week to get her back in the air." He caressed the airplane's propeller as he spoke, "Rotten time to go on the fritz, old girl."

"We haven't got a week," Lily had desperation sneaking into her eyes. "There must be another plane and a pilot we can hire?"

Otto's eyes grew another rim around their sockets. "Croxford, your friend, Penny, might be available. He does sightseeing flights for tourists in his amphibian, ma'am. Hell of a pilot when you consider the hours he's logged without killing anyone, with the exception of Germans, that is. Penny won medals flying fighters for the RAF. In fact, I believe he was an ace. Am I right, Croxford?"

"He was indeed an ace," Rigby acknowledged.

"Thought so. I hate losing the business, but it looks like Penny's your man."

Lily asked, "Where can we find him?"

"Your timing couldn't be better. That's Penny on final approach." He pointed at a Cessna-185 amphibian touching down at the northern end of the runway.

"And ma'am, don't let Penny's advanced age frighten you. He's forgotten more about flying than I'll ever know."

Rigby said, "Thanks, Otto. Get this crate fixed. I need you as backup."

"You know how to reach me. Tell Penny I recommended him."

"You bet. Cheers."

Colonel Harold Pennington was awarded the Distinguished Flying Cross for flying spitfires against the Luftwaffe in the Battle of Britain. Penny was well into his eighties. His face bore scars from two airplane crashes including the loss of an eye. Thick glasses magnified both his good eye and the glass one. What little hair he had was snow white and without any direction. He wore hearing aids in both ears. A pitted bulbous nose indicated a life of heavy consumption. His neck refused to straighten, which gave him the appearance of a one-eyed inquisitive goose. To their surprise, Penny climbed down from the amphibian's cockpit with the agility of a vervet monkey. When he saw Rigby, he smiled and shook hands. His grip is still rock-solid, Rigby thought.

"Afternoon, Penny," Rigby said carefully enunciating the words. "Say, we'd like to hire your airplane."

Penny cupped his ear. "What? Well, of course, I'm bloody tired. Why wouldn't I be, I've been flying all day!"

Rigby spoke again. This time he mouthed the words more visibly. "I said... we'd like to charter your seaplane."

"I beg your pardon?" Penny adjusted the volume control on his hearing aids. Rigby repeated the offer a third time. "What? Why the hell didn't you say so? I get a thousand rand per diem plus fuel and expenses."

Lily blurted, "We'll take it." She nodded to authenticate her acceptance.

"For how many days?" Penny cocked his head a little straighter than normal.

"Let's say ten and I'll you pay in advance," Lily said.

"Jolly good." Penny interlocked his fingers and cracked his boney knuckles. "What's our destination?"

Rigby said, "Mozambique and then north until we find what we're looking for."

Penny pulled his earlobe thinking, what are they up to? The mention of money seemed to improve his hearing. He gnawed on his furled lip for a second and then in a quiet voice inquired, "Number of passengers and departure date? Say, what was your name again?"

"Lillian Rosen. How about tomorrow morning?" Rigby interjected. "There'll be three of us."

"So, it's four plus essentials. I reckon she can handle the load." Penny thumped his fist on the seaplane's float.

Penny addressed Lily grinning "You know, Miss Rosen, you should be more careful about the company you keep."

"With friends like you, who needs bloody enemies?" Rigby joked.

Penny's grin vanished in a flash. "Right. Now, give me the details."

Lily and Rigby didn't sugarcoat their objective. They told him everything. Lily even showed him the execution photographs. Penny listened intently, asking questions, but not raising obstacles.

After they had finished speaking, Penny retrieved a flask from his hip pocket and took a long chug. When he noticed Lily's concern, he announced, "Don't worry—I only nip when I'm on *terra firma*. Helps settle my fiddly stomach. Now, where was I? Oh, let's not split atoms here. We might find ourselves in the shit. If things get dicey, not being armed would be a major cock-up. Croxford, I've got something I'd like to show you."

Penny broke out some tools. He unscrewed the top hatch-covers sealing the amphibian's floats. Each float contained a hidden watertight compartment. "A man could smuggle two dozen Kalashnikovs in these floats, if he had a mind to," Penny stated a little too loudly and added proudly, "And I have, more than once. I must tell you in all honesty, I never felt a sense of impropriety about my transgressions. My unsavory British ancestry, no doubt."

"Has to be. Otto says you're a legend among smugglers," Rigby said grinning.

Penny returned his grin. "Did he now? Truth be known, Otto's arrest record for smuggling would make a hardened criminal envious. I've had my share of run-ins. It makes life more interesting. Wouldn't you agree, Croxford?"

"Anything you say, Penny."

Lily interrupted. "Are those bullet holes?" She pointed at a line of aluminum patches on the fuselage.

Penny smiled. "They are indeed bullet holes. Mr. Croxford drafted me and my Cessna for recon flights to help him with his anti-poaching patrols. It seems some people in this country do not share his enthusiasm for our wildlife."

Lily said, "What time tomorrow? Oh, before I forget, maybe you should hide this."

JAMES GARDNER

She retrieved a Walther PPK from her purse and handed the pistol to Rigby who fondled the weapon before giving it to Penny. Rigby and Penny glanced at each other.

"I travel in some of the poorest countries in the world. It's my security blanket," Lily said. "A girl can't be too careful."

Penny seemed to accept her explanation, but a voice deep inside Rigby raised the hair on the back of his neck. Penny handed the pistol back to her. "Keep this in your purse. We might need it in a pinch."

Penny said, "Let's be off before sunrise. No sense alerting airport security. I plan to follow the Zambezi River to the coastline. It's not as a crow flies, but it does give us options if we have an engine failure." When Penny saw Lily's panic, he amended his remark. "Didn't mean to give you the jitters. It's just a much more scenic route, actually."

Rigby said to Penny, "See you before first light."

"Toodaloo," Penny slurred. He upended his flask draining the last drop, came to attention and saluted.

As they drove away from the airport, Lily said to Rigby, "Our pilot's older than dirt. And what's with his drinking? I was worried about North Africa. Now, I'm praying we make it that far."

"I wouldn't worry about Penny. And as far as his drinking goes, his consumption pales by comparison to my own." Seeing her apprehension made him laugh.

She chewed on a hangnail. "Great. Now, I feel much better."

They rode in silence for a few minutes.

Rigby's grin eroded. He stared straight ahead and asked, "Lily, what's with the concealed weapon?"

"Like I said, I travel in third-world countries. In case you've forgotten, we Jews are sometimes targeted by the crazies. Lily changed the subject. "By the way, who's our fourth?"

"A black Zimbabwean. We fought together in the bush war. I may have mentioned Jedediah. I trust Jed as much as any man I've ever known. You'll like him."

Lily said, "I remember your mentioning a Sam. Whatever happened to him?"

Rigby sighed deeply. "He was killed in a lion-hunting accident in Mozambique. The second worse day in my life."

Lily lowered her eyes. "I'm sorry." After hesitating she asked, "Does anyone ever die from natural causes in this country?"

"Not many. Hope I do. Although, the way my life's going lately, I doubt I'll make it."

Lily stared at the passing bush veldt. Without looking over, she said, "Funny how things turned out. Ever wonder what might have happened if we'd stayed together?"

"Can't say I haven't thought about it. Not sure you would've been happy here.

Lily manufactured a disbelieving expression. "Oh, what do you base that on?"

"Africa is hard on women. It takes someone special."

"You mean someone like Helen?" She tried hard, but couldn't hide the irritation in her voice.

"Huxley said it best, 'Africa is a cruel continent. She takes your heart and grinds it into powder. Warts and all, Helen loved Africa and Africans, for that matter."

She looked over at him. "Didn't Bishop Tutu say that white people sent missionaries to Africa bearing Bibles? They told Africans to close their eyes and pray? When the natives opened their eyes they had the Bibles, but the whites had their land?"

"I wouldn't quote Tutu, if I were you. Rhodesia had one of the highest standards of living in the world. Now, Zimbabwe is so broke it may never recover. Blacks have suffered the most."

"Tutu won the Nobel Peace Prize."

"So did the American president. It's a joke."

She sighed. "It all seems so pointless. These people have taken everything from you. How can you ever forgive them?"

"One man's crime doesn't condemn an entire country." He explained that as a descendant of the first white settlers, he felt responsible for his country's future. "Zimbabweans are great people ruled by a retched government."

"I wish I had your capacity to forgive," she said and added, "Are you sure you're being honest with yourself."

"I'm not sure about anything these days, Lily."

They fell into a thoughtful silence.

Lily smiled inwardly. So far, her plan was working right on schedule.

As Christine watched her father and Lily climb out of the Land Rover, she felt unsettled. She knew they would be leaving in a few

JAMES GARDNER

days or maybe even sooner.

There was something odd about Lily Rosen. Something she couldn't put her finger on and now it was too late to do anything about it. "How'd it go?"

"Everything went great," Rigby replied.

"Lily, you must excuse my father. He's been inoculated against many basic human frailties, like self-doubt and fear, for instance."

He ignored his daughter's jab. "We leave in the morning. To save time, we chartered Harold Pennington's airplane."

"That's great." Christine's unenthusiastic eyes conflicted with her reply.

Lily broke the awkwardness. "Let's go out for dinner. It'll be my treat. What about one of the hotels in town?"

"You two go. I've got rounds to make." Christine turned on her heel.

Rigby also begged off.

The sky was grey and the clouds were building as Rigby drove to Jedediah's village. An old African proverb says, "If wealth was the inevitable result of backbreaking labor, then every African woman would be a millionaire." Working from sunrise to sunset, Jed's five wives were not exceptions to this rule. Mostly, they toiled in the maize fields bending at impossible angles, planting corn kernels and weeding. By the time Rigby arrived at the village, Jed's women were either tending children or preparing a corn porridge with the consistency of *Papier Mache*. Idle men, inspired by vast quantities of sorghum beer, pontificated under a grass-thatched central hut.

Scrawny chickens scavenged in black dirt festooned by garbage between the huts. Pot-bellied boys played soccer with a half-deflated ball. The girls helped their mothers. The village gave off a pleasant charred smoky odor.

Jed's face lit up when he saw Rigby drive up. Even though they were old friends, strict greeting customs had to be adhered to. Older Africans call white men *Baba*, the equivalent of father as a sign of respect. "I see you, *Baba*. How is your daughter's health?" Jed inquired. Jed's infant son had a hangdog look locked on his dirty face. He hugged his father's knees and peeked around at Rigby. The bashful boy was wide-eyed and naked. Two streaks of shiny snot stained his upper lip. Flies crawled around his nostrils and eyes. He picked his nose and ate the prize with one hand and pulled his penis with the other hand.

"Christine is good." Rigby took mental inventory. Does he have four or five wives, he wondered. "Are your wives well?"

Jed sighed resignedly. "Well enough, considering they are spoiled by their foolish husband. Can I offer you beer or perhaps some palm wine?"

"*Waita Zuaka*. Beer would be brilliant," Rigby said, clapping his hands as a traditional sign of gratitude.

Jed barked at his wives in Shona. One of his wives ran over and scooped up the child. Another wife handed Rigby a bottle of homemade beer. Both women avoided eye contact. Jed's senior wife, exempt of such formalities, yelled, "*Mhoro, Baba*." Rigby returned the woman's greeting. He turned to Jed saying, "I have work for us."

Jed looked solemn. "What kind of work."

"Has old age made you fussy?"

"We are both old." Jed thought for moment and then he said pensively, "Last night, I dreamed we would make a long journey together. We were riding on the wings of a fish eagle."

Rigby said, "We are hired to rescue a woman. The work has danger. If you are willing, we must leave before the sun rises."

On the surface, Jed's response sounded almost noncommittal, but inwardly he trembled from exhilaration, like a hunting dog on point. "A man can drown in calm water. I'll be waiting for you, *Baba*."

The shook hands and parted company.

14

It was pitch-black when Rigby, Lily and Jed arrived at the airfield. Penny had already fueled his airplane. Rigby parked his Land Rover next to the amphibian. His headlights illuminated a fish eagle painted on the Cessna's rudder. After loading the baggage, everyone climbed onboard. Penny taxied the overloaded Cessna to the end of the runway. It was a silky smooth takeoff. His long boney fingers moved over the controls like the solo pianist playing a concerto. He coaxed the forty-year-old bird into a stubborn climb, leveled off and then banked gingerly into the first silvery glow of dawn. The shining mist above Victoria Falls promised the sun, but the mighty Zambezi was still only a darkened void as it snaked like a serpent toward the Indian Ocean. Cooking fires identified native villages, but most of what was beneath them was obscured by ground fog and haze.

Gradually, the dawn dissolved into a flawless azure sky. They flew over Lake Kariba. The windless morning gave the water a polished-black-marble look. The lake was dotted with Tonga kapenta fishing boats brimming with the night's catch. Some boats were moored against rickety wooden docks for offloading.

Penny yelled at Rigby over the groaning engine. "Otto told me he gave you flying lessons."

"That's right. Ten years ago in the Sudan. We were taking ground-fire from the Arabs. Otto figured it was only a matter of time before one of us got shot. He wanted to make sure I could fly if he was the unlucky one to get hit."

Penny rubbed his eyelid. "Take the controls, Croxford. I've got some dirt in my peeper." He popped out his glass-eye, stuck it his mouth and rolled it between his cheeks. After rinsing it with saliva, he polished the glass-eye on his shirt. He reinserted the eyeball and looked over at Rigby. Penny winked his working eye. "How do I look?"

"Penny, you look like a movie star," Rigby answered. "In fact, I'd say you look absolutely stunning."

"Think I'll snooze. Wake me if something startling happens."

"Jesus, Penny, I'm not sure about this," Rigby said panicking. "What constitutes startling?"

"Say, we hit something large, like a dirigible for instance. Don't worry. As they say, it's like riding a bicycle. Follow the river and keep her at three grand. Too high is much preferred over too low." Penny's smile broadened. "The first principle of flight is a healthy respect for altitude."

The Cessna shot up five-hundred feet and then nosedived down to three thousand feet. It was like riding a rollercoaster.

Penny smacked Rigby's hands like a Catholic nun striking a misbehaving schoolboy. "For God's sake, you're gripping the yoke like it was a bloody sledgehammer. Pretend you're holding your tallywacker taking a pee. I thought you said you could fly."

"I never said I was a pilot." Rigby glanced back at Lily and Jed, both were dozing. Little by little, the altitude changes became less violent. Penny patted Rigby's shoulder. "Much better. Now, you've got it. Wake me in an hour."

JAMES GARDNER

Within seconds, Penny was snoring peacefully. His glass eye remained transfixed and unmoving. Within minutes, a long silver string of dribble hung from his lower lip.

Rigby rubbed the back of his hand across his forehead and then wiped the sweat on his shirt. As he got reacquainted with flying, his mind drifted. *No matter how this plays out, I'm glad I agreed to help her.* He'd done his duty and felt good about himself. *Something feels different this time. Helen's death has changed me. Maybe this is how it all ends,* he thought.

One hour later, Penny woke up from his catnap. He yawned scanning the flight instruments. "Lovely work, Croxford. I've got her." He took the yoke and descended into a sandstone sided gorge etched by the zigzagging Zambezi. At times, they were only a few feet above the river, which was now benign. They flushed flocks of open-billed storks, white egrets and pairs of Egyptian geese. Lily squealed at the sight of elephants and pods of hippos. Jed was mesmerized. Penny pointed at crocodiles basking on a sandbar and a giraffe standing on splayed legs drinking at the water's edge. "Oops," Penny shouted as he ascended over a flushed giant blue heron.

As Rigby fumbled for his sunglasses, he found a handwritten note folded over a page torn from a medical textbook. The note read:

Daddy dearest,

I don't trust your newfound friend. She should be able to answer the basic medical questions I've underlined. If she can't, she's not who she claims to be.

Be careful. I love you.

Christine

He stuffed his daughter's note back into his breast pocket and glanced back at Lily. She was still so preoccupied with the heron near-miss, she didn't notice. Normally, he would discount the warning as a daughter's petty jealousy. But like her mother, Christine possessed a sixth sense. When the time is right I need to confront Lily, he thought.

Penny studied the topography and then he referred to an aeronautical chart. "The Kariba airfield's around here someplace. It damn better be—we're about to run out of fuel."

Lily shouted into Penny's hearing aid. "Are you saying we're lost, Colonel Pennington?" She smiled briefly, but was too close to panic to hold the smile for more than a split second.

He scanned the horizon. "I prefer saying that the airport had been temporarily misplaced. Believe it or not, Ms. Rosen, I've been flying in Africa for quite some time. And I've been "lost" as you so bluntly put it, many times. It's what makes bush flying such jolly good fun."

"I'm not laughing, Colonel." Lily said. "This isn't funny."

A clearing in the trees came into view. Penny pointed. "There's our misplaced airfield."

"I still don't see it." Lily shaded her eyes. "Don't tell me you mean that dirt road?"

"What did you expect, Jan Smuts International? Better fasten your seatbelts. This could get very interesting."

Penny overflew the airport. After locating a tattered windsock, he turned back into the wind. He made a last minute correction to avoid a pothole and touched down as delicately as a dragonfly landing on a pond. "So, Ms. Rosen, are you happy now?"

Lily exhaled. "Ask me again in ten days."

"Our next fuel stop is Tete. That's where we clear Mozambican customs." He peered over the top of his repaired glasses at Rigby and rolled his working eye. "Things could get a bit dicey. Let's do our doubly best to act like tourists, shall we."

Penny refueled the aircraft. They stretched their legs and used the loo. Everyone climbed back onboard. Penny taxied out to the end of the dirt strip. After a quick magneto check, he fire-walled his amphibian. The old Cessna sputtered once and roared down the runway. He lifted off into the hot midday heat and set a bumpy easterly course for the Indian Ocean. Penny found cooler air and less turbulence at fifty-five hundred feet.

The land moving beneath them was spotted by teak trees, mopani scrub and a few lonely baobabs. Occasional granite outcroppings marked the earth like moles on an old woman's face. Mozambique had suffered through a long civil war. Poaching had eradicated the country's wildlife. From time to time, they spotted small herds of domestic cattle, but mostly it was as lifeless as the moon.

Penny touched Rigby to rouse him. "Every time I fly into Mozambique, I think about our war and Operation Eland. By God, those were the days. That was our finest hour, I dare say."

Rigby nodded without much enthusiasm and gave Penny a halfhearted fist-bump. He leaned his head against the window, closed his eyes and fell into a shallow sleep. A vision flashed before his mind's eye. He revisited his Selous Scout selection ceremony. One hundred volunteers had been whittled down to only ten recruits.

Thanks to Penny's reminiscing, his dreaming switched to the incursion into Mozambique during the Bush War.

At the time, Operation Eland was said to have too many moving parts not to be concocted by a madman. Eighty-four Selous Scouts traveling in fourteen armored trucks would attack a guerilla camp harboring five thousand terrorists. Our commander motivated us by recounting that the terrorists' landmines were maiming our woman and children. Our mission was to wreak havoc. To say we were successful that day was understated. I remember the adrenalin rush. It was a beautiful Sunday morning. Five thousand unarmed recruits had gathered on a parade ground to hear what they thought would be a political speech. Our camouflaged trucks lined up in a perfect cross-fire killing zone. What they heard was the deep throaty roar from our twenty-millimeter machineguns. The parade ground was littered with dead and dying men. And then our mad dash back across the border. It happened years ago, but I can still hear their screams.

South African newspapers tallied the final score; one thousand terrorists killed versus one dead Rhodesian. Operation Eland was hailed a monumental victory by Rhodesia's High Command. London newspapers called it a massacre. I wish I could erase the memory.

Rigby tried to untangle himself from the grip of the nightmare.

He opened his eyes and remembered where he was and what he was doing. A drop of sweat hung from the tip of his nose.

Penny patted Rigby's arm and apologized. "Sorry, old friend. I didn't mean to give you the combat sweats."

Leaning back his head, Rigby closed his eyes. "War is such a bloody curse. Saber rattlers never see teenage soldiers holding in their guts."

"Quite right. If I live to be a hundred, I'll never stop having the most dreadful nightmares," Penny admitted.

"We did dreadful things. Nightmares are God's punishment for the sins we committed."

Penny swallowed hard. "I reckon so."

JAMES GARDNER

15

Mozambique

They landed at the Tete Airport as planned. The terminal building was a shack fronted by a sagging porch in need of repairs. Penny filled out the required travel documents under the watchful eye of a roly-poly customs agent who spoke Portuguese. He was so neckless, his earlobes rested on his shoulders. The man removed his sunglasses and hung the ear-frame from the corner of his mouth. He stamped their passports. Lily paid the landing fee. Everything seemed to be running smoothly, but then the customs agent took an interest in Penny's amphibian. When he thumped his knuckles on the airplane's amphibious floats, Rigby pretended to find something on the ground. "Sir, did you drop this?" Rigby handed the man a five-hundred rand note, which represented a month's salary. The man checked for onlookers, before tucking the money into his pocket. *"Ben-vindo a Mozambique,"* the agent announced welcoming them to Mozambique.

Penny had them airborne in ten minutes. "So far, so good," he said crossing his fingers.

Lily leaned over the front seat and spoke into Rigby's ear. "You were right about the border guards."

"No stigma attached to accepting bribes in Africa," he explained.

Penny shouted, "When we see the ocean, I move we call it a day. Spend the night. Rest up and the like. I say we've earned a libation or two." He involuntarily licked his lips. "It's a long way to Tanzania. Hopefully, we can make Dar es Salaam in two full days. The port's a layover for Arab dhows working the coast." Penny glanced back at Lily. "If your ex-husband's yacht came within a thousand kilometers, those bloody Arabs will know about it. Anyway, for what it's worth, that's my suggestion."

No one argued.

Penny opted for a water-landing on the Bons Sinais River. Swept by an outgoing tide, the milky-tea colored river fouled the ocean for as far as the naked eye could see. Penny scanned the proposed landing spot for floating debris. He pointed at a single file of brown pelicans flaring to land. An anchored dhow weather cocking confirmed the wind direction. Penny pulled in twenty degrees of flaps and retarded the throttle. "Brace yourselves. You're about to have the most fun you can have with your clothes on." Seconds later he shouted, "Touchdown!" as the seaplane's floats gently kissed the water.

Lily patted Penny's shoulder. "Hurrah! Otto was right. You are the best."

"Glad you approve, Miss Lily."

Penny water-taxied into a marshy lagoon and anchored his amphibian. Nesting cormorants and roseate spoonbills had whitened the mangroves with their droppings. Out of nowhere, a flotilla of tiny boats surrounded Penny's amphibian. Women selling curios hocked their wares. A skinny man offered to guard the seaplane, which Penny agreed to.

They waded ashore at the edge of town. Rigby took Jed aside and said, "See what you can find out from the locals."

Like most post-colonial African cities, this one had fallen on hard times. What had been picturesque fifty years ago was now dilapidated. Portuguese colonialists yielded to the black majority in a fifteen-year civil war. This once vibrant port city was now a sad collection of crumbling buildings and boarded-up stores. Some structures still bore the pock-marks from artillery shells. The sour stench of human waste battled against the fragrances from cooking fires. A boy pushed a crippled woman in a wheelbarrow, the equivalent of an African wheelchair. Gawkers stared. Beggars swarmed them. Vultures and black crows waited in the trees. The city looked desperate, but the people, like most Africans, appeared content.

The Leao Hotel was a perfect fit. The signage had letters missing. The dirty brown exterior walls were crisscrossed by improvised electrical wiring. An abandoned satellite dish served as a planter for struggling black violets. Wobbly ceiling fans amplified the humid air when the electricity worked, which was intermittent. Some windows had panes missing.

After checking in, Penny joked, "One needs a sense of humor while traveling in Africa. Let's say sundowners in one hour at the patio bar."

Rigby headed back to the waterfront to find Jed. They met each other in the middle of the town. Jed had nothing to report. An army of feral children followed them as they walked the streets. Cajoling prostitutes solicited business from the windows. A heavyset woman pulled up her skirt. When they ignored her, she yelled something in Portuguese. There wasn't a need for a translator.

Lily knocked on Penny's hotel-room door. "Do you have hot water?"

"I'm encouraged to hear we have water, hot or cold. Hope you weren't expecting the Savoy."

Lily said, "I've never seen such poverty. I weep for these people. God take pity on their poor souls."

"I'm afraid I've shed so many tears for Zimbabweans, I have nothing left," Penny said.

"Can I ask you a question?" Lily asked.

He held up a hand to stop her. His hearing aid emitted a shill whistle. After adjusting the volume, he said, "Make it an easy one. I'm afraid old age has diminished my mental acuity."

"How well do you know Rigby?"

"I suspect, better than anyone alive with the exception of his late wife. Most women are devoted to men who don't deserve their loyalty, and I include myself in that company. In his case, the devotion was warranted. Our friend's got the qualities all men aspire for and very few possess. You know about his war record. He witnessed things no man should see."

"He seems well adjusted, considering."

"I bet you didn't know that Helen came from money? Rigby inherited her fortune, but he disclaimed the inheritance. He claimed the money would be a nail in his coffin."

"I had no idea."

"Lily, would you mind cutting to the chase?"

"Which is...?" she asked.

"Do you have a future with him?" He answered a little too loudly. She recoiled slightly. He adjusted his hearing aid volume again.

Lily looked embarrassed, but nodded reluctantly and then she said, "You certainly don't pull any punches, do you?"

"At my age? You've got some heavy lifting to do. He revered Helen. Hope I don't sound too discouraging. They were exact polar opposites. She was a bleeding heart liberal. He was an anachronistic warrior. Somehow their marriage worked like a Swiss watch."

"Your optimism is overwhelming."

"You asked me," he reminded her.

"I know." She gathered her thoughts. "The important thing is to find my daughter. After that, let the chips fall where they may." She walked to the door. "Thanks for being honest with me, Penny."

"You're quite welcome, my dear. See you at the bar."

The hotel's swimming pool contained stringy clops of green algae. The bartender was a hatchet-faced man sporting a thin Clark-Gable mustache. His nose was engraved with blackheads. His pallor said he seldom ventured outdoors. He nipped the stub of a cigarette between his long dirty fingernails, stifled a phlegm-induced rattle, and announced, "What's your pleasure, folks?" An oscillating fan provided them with sinus-clearing periodic whiffs of the bartender. He smelled like sour milk and stale tobacco.

Seeing the chalky cocktail glasses, Lily said, "A beer would be lovely." She felt the man's eyes exploring her body. "You can save the glass."

Penny and Rigby also ordered beers.

"I take it, you're all from Zimbabwe?" he asked, recognizing Rigby's accent. He smacked a horsefly with a swatter and swept it off the bar.

"That's right," answered Rigby.

"I hear Zim's a beastly mess. Not that we're much better off, or the whole of Africa for that matter. What brings you to Mozambique, if you don't mind me asking? 'Ope I ain't prying," He flashed them a yellow-toothed grin.

Everyone looked at Rigby. "We're on holiday, actually."

Sure you are. And I'm the next king of England, he thought. He shook a cigarette out of his pack and squinted as he lit it. Exhaling the smoke through his nostrils, he said, "Of course, it ain't none of my business, is it?"

"We could ask you the same question," Lily said

He made a finger-rubbing gesture of money. "That one's easy enough. Living here is cheap and so are the ladies."

He glanced at a light-complexioned, full-bosomed woman sitting alone at the end of the bar. Her distinguishing feature was a large mole on her upper lip. "I'm a military pensioner. Can't afford anything fancy, mind you. Spent thirty years in Burma and India with the British army, I did. Can't say I'm fond of munts, but Mozambican women are a step up."

"Did I see a Mosque in town?" Lily asked him.

"Yes, ma'am. Arab and Portuguese slave-traders built this city. Next to Zanzibar, this was the biggest slave port in East Africa."

Lily said, "Thank God, that's behind us. I mean slavery."

Rigby challenged her. "I'm embarrassed to admit slavery hasn't ended in Africa—another one of our dirty little secrets exposed."

Penny added, "Slaves make up ten percent of the population in some countries."

Lily said, "It doesn't seem possible. Not in this day and age. What happened to God?"

"When it comes to Africa, God's on holiday," Rigby mentioned.

A pitiless smile curled the bartender's lips. "Arabs ran the slave trade here for over a thousand years. Black beauties for their harems, mostly. The male slaves were castrated. Afraid of the black seed, I bet. Can't say I blame them much."

Lily started to speak, but Rigby stopped her with a look.

The bartender addressed Penny. "Sir, you strike me as a military man." He squashed his cigarette butt in an overflowing ashtray.

Penny eyed the barkeep's mistress as he spoke. She looked back at him with eyes revealing the hopelessness of her reality. "I was an officer in His Majesty's Royal Air Force. Played a minor role in the air battle over Britain."

"Minor role? That's a laugh. He was an ace," Rigby stated looking at Penny.

The bartender clicked his heels together and saluted. "I'm honored to meet you, sir. Hard to believe I'm sharing sundowners with a war hero."

Penny swiveled his head allowing him to focus his working eye on the man. He waved a hand dismissively. "Say, maybe you *can* help us. We're looking for a friend, actually.

He's vacationing on his yacht, the Black Cygnet. He was last seen off Djibouti or thereabouts. There's a chance he might have made it this far south."

The bartender poured himself another jigger of Irish whiskey, guzzled it and licked his mustache. "Ain't my favorite place in the world, Djibouti, rather the reverse. Banditos are as thick as flies on camel shit. Pardon me, miss. If your friend made it to Mozambique, I'd know about it. I ain't seen hide nor hair of him."

"You're sure about that?"

He squeezed a blackhead and examined the discharge. "Uh-huh."

Rigby asked him, "What year did you say you settled here?"

The bartender shot back with, "I don't think I take your meaning, sir." He knew Rigby's question was meant to find out which side he backed in Mozambique's civil war.

Rigby probed further. "I led military incursions into this country during the Rhodesian Bush War. Thought we might have crossed paths." He tried to engage the man's gaze, but was unsuccessful.

The bartender stared at Lily, drinking her in as he spoke. "Oh, I doubt that's possible," He gave Rigby a nervous glance before changing the subject. It was a card he meant to keep close to his chest. "Will you be dining with us tonight, governor? My woman does the cooking when she's not tended to her more important duties." He smirked suggestively.

"Are there any other restaurants in town?" Rigby asked hopefully.

The bartender crackled, "*Nenhum.*"

"Can I see a menu?" Lily asked.

"No need. We're serving tiger prawns tonight and every night, ma'am. You can have them sautéed, fried, boiled, baked or raw if you prefer. That's the whole enchilada, as they say. " His visual frisk lingered on her breasts.

Lily felt her scalp tighten. "Well then, I guess I'll try the prawns."

"Good choice, ma'am."

"I'm up for a run before dinner. Any takers?" Lily looked at Rigby, who shook his head and saluted her with his beer.

Minutes later, Lily reappeared wearing jogging shoes, skintight shorts and a loose-fitting halter top. The deep cleavage in her heart-shaped buttocks separated two perfectly rounded spheres. Her legs were muscular. Veins in her biceps defined her as a weightlifter. The bartender's stare raked her from head to toe. Rigby gave her a second glance and waved as she exited the hotel.

The bartender said to Rigby, "I take it she's your woman? And a fine specimen she is, I might add."

"She's just a good friend."

The bartender swatted a mosquito on the back of his neck. "Is she now? Reminds me of a Melanesian gal I used to shag. Tits like coconuts. As fit as a fiddle and great in the sack. Ran off with a munt, she did. He was blacker than tar. Hard to figure." The impropriety of making suggestive comparisons about Lily seemed totally lost on the man.

Rigby ignored his crudeness. Turning to Penny, he said, "I need to freshen up."

"Righto, old chap. Think I'll do the same," Penny indicated.

They left without saying goodbye to the barkeep. As soon as they were out of earshot, Rigby spoke to Penny in barely an audible voice, "Everything about him is wrong."

"My thoughts precisely," agreed Penny.

Rigby said, "The English can be mental. Probably inbreeding, I dare say."

Penny observed half-jokingly, "For God's sake, Croxford, he's no Englishman. That sloping forehead. The unintelligent eyes. Those protruding ears. Why, he's as Irish as Paddy's pig, pure and simple."

Rigby glanced back scratching his head. "Whatever he is, I doubt the man has ever drawn an honest breath. Probably choke to death if he did."

"From your lips to God's ears," Penny said.

The bartender locked the barroom door behind them. He dialed his mobile phone. When a man answered he said, "I was told you'd pay good money for information about anyone making inquiries about the vessel, the Black Cygnet. If such be a consideration, how much will you pay and how can I get it?"

"Yes, I'll hold the line."

Lily jogged down a narrow dirt road lined by square shacks made from sheets of corrugated metal in various states of rusting decay.

A motley assortment of gawking men stared at her as she ran past them. Raggedly dressed children waved. Dogs yapped incessantly. One hollow-bellied mongrel took up the chase. Lily cut down a path paralleling the shoreline with the dog in hot pursuit. The mangroves purpled and the mud blackened in the fading light. Swallows chasing insects streaked the sky. When she ratcheted up her pace the mongrel gave up. Wading birds took flight. The insidious cicada concert was silenced. Hermit crabs scurried back into their mud-holes. A sentinel baboon barked an alarm. She glanced at her watch and broke into a sprint for the last ten minutes.

That's enough, she thought slowing back down to a jog. On the way back she found the dog with his tongue hanging out. "What's wrong, boy, too fast for you?" He wagged his tail and trotted after her. Thirty minutes had passed since Lily started her run. The sun dipped below the horizon. Looking into the mangroves, she saw glowing eyes.

The distant giggling of hyenas carried on the wind. She shivered. After stumbling in the dark a few times, she bent down and whispered to the mongrel, "C'mon boy, show me the way home." They set off into the night.

In spite of a moonless night, Lily managed to find her hotel's backdoor. She bent over trying to slow down her pulse. She started to open the door, but hesitated. She heard sobbing.

Lily found a woman hiding between two dustbins. "Are you hurt?" Lily asked. The woman didn't answer. Lily gently lifted the woman's chin to the light. Her face was bruised and battered. One eye was swollen shut. Blood caked her nostrils. It was the bartender's African mistress.

The backdoor swung open. Light illuminated a large man standing in the door well. "Why, you good for nothing kaffir, I'll teach you. I..."

The woman cowered. When he saw Lily standing in the shadows he stopped dead in his tracks. "This ain't your business, lady. It's between me and her. You better leave before I lose my temper." He redirected his fury on the skinny mongrel. He picked up a stone and hurled it. "Get, you flea-bitten cur." The dog flinched, but it didn't bolt.

Lily stepped out of the shadows. Instead of showing fear, she smiled seductively and coaxed him closer. Confused, he returned her smile and moved toward her. She pulled his head down, pecked his cheek and blew suggestively into his ear. Lust trumped caution. Lily had the edge she needed.

I knew it. Bugger all, she's a goddamn nympho, he told himself.

Lily turned around, pulled down her shorts and presented her bare rump to him.

He fumbled with his zipper. "Why hell, doggy style is my middle name."

He grunted. She felt his misaimed semi-erection bump against her thigh. Lily stepped forward and turned sideways. Her sidekick was perfectly timed and on target. He grabbed his testicles and doubled over. His blood-curdling screech sounded more animal than human. She jockeyed for a better angle and drove a flying elbow into his temple. He swayed dizzily for a split second before dropping to his knees. The dropkick to his face could have propelled a rugby ball a hundred meters. He rolled up into a fetal position. Lily flipped him over and sat down on his chest. Blood infused sobbing bubbled from his lips. Their faces almost touched. "Stop moaning, you fucking crybaby. You listen to me, you *shtik drek*. The next time you beat a woman I want you to remember me and what I did to you."

Lily stood up. She rubbed the soreness out of her elbow and righted her shorts. She acted like the assault was nothing more

JAMES GARDNER

than a minor inconvenience. Her eyes were filled with hostility, but they softened as she addressed the woman. "You speak English?" The woman nodded. "He's all yours. Do what you want to him." She ran over and kissed Lily's hand.

The mongrel dog sniffed, cocked up his leg and urinated on the man's arm.

One hour later, the group met for dinner. It had been a long day. The atmosphere was subdued. The dialogue was mostly monosyllabic. Their table conversation focused on the highlights of the flight. Penny touched on what was ahead. Both Penny and Rigby raised questions about the bartender's absence, but Lily never mentioned her violent encounter. During dinner she kept touching Rigby's arm. Her flirtations were not missed by Jed. Penny wanted an early departure. Everyone retired to his respective room.

Rigby searched his room for Christine's note, but he couldn't find it.

He opened the adjoining door and found Jed listening to a radio. Before he could speak, Jed said, "I have been waiting for you, Baba. You are troubled about the woman."

"What're you talking about?" Rigby asked unconvincingly. He had witnessed Jed's clairvoyance many times. Jed may have been uneducated, but he was never underestimated.

"Beware of the black widow spider. She eats her mate after they couple. It would be wise to move slowly with this woman."

Rigby was taken aback. He reiterated his daughter's warning. "Like you, Christine doesn't think Lily's on the up-and-up. What's your opinion?"

"Women are never trustworthy," Jed replied thoughtfully.

"Why have five wives if you can't trust them?" Rigby asked.

"A question I have asked myself many times. I believe in one God, but one wife is unholy. The whites take many wives, one after another. Can you explain the difference?"

Rigby couldn't think of a logical reply. He mulled Jed's question for a full minute before ignoring it. "Of course, it could be Christine's imagination. Or she's being overly protective. In her case, jealousy is a forgivable sin."

Jed blurted out of nowhere, "Will you take this woman as a wife?"

Rigby's face registered total shock. "What? Don't be absurd. I have no such intentions."

Jed appeared unconvinced.

"Take her as my *wife*? You must be joking. Goodnight, you old coffin-dodger." The remark made Jed grin, but only momentarily.

Rigby left the room and closed the door.

Rigby wasn't surprised to find Lily in his bed, but he acted like he was. She was wearing a red nightgown. Her long legs were folded lotus style. She patted the bed inviting him to join her. The smell of her made him lightheaded. A ceiling fan cast spinning shadows on her face. Waves crashing on the beach made soft sighs. He resisted the allure of her suggestive smile. He felt blood rushing into his extremities. "Lily..., I can't."

Lily took a few moments to digest his unexpected rejection.

The faint quiver of her lips indicated humiliation. She let the wounded look drop from her face and looked deeply into his eyes.

She got up from the bed, walked out onto the balcony and looked up into the star-glutted inky sky. A few wispy clouds skated across the moon. The silvery luminescence from moonshine danced on the curls of incoming waves. With her back turned, she said, "I meant what I said about you being the best man I ever knew. I always tried to imagine what it would be like being Mrs. Rigby Croxford. For what it's worth, I was never with a man that I didn't pretend it was you. God, I can't believe I admitted that." Lily blushed secretly. A faraway look came into her eyes. "The truth is—I'm not good enough for you. I never was. I've done terrible things in my life. Things I'm not proud of."

"God knows, I've got my crosses to bear, we all do. The last thing in the world I wanted to do was to hurt you. I hope you know that. I'm flattered beyond belief." He walked over, grabbed her hand and kissed it. "Forgive me?"

"Of course." She took a deep breath and kissed his cheek. "I can wait. Besides, isn't patience considered a virtue?"

He nodded his answer. Lily touched his lips with her finger to prevent him from speaking and left his room.

After she closed the door, he exhaled a long audible sigh.

James Gardner

16

The flight to Dar es Salaam

Penny followed the coastline north. It was savanna woodlands inland and a monotonous shoreline congested by millions of coconut trees interrupted by a few ephemeral rivers and the rusty hulks of shipwrecks. Bleached pearl-white sand-dunes were dotted by grassy patches. The crystal clear waters of the Indian Ocean reflected a turquoise-colored sky. Coral reefs formed breakwaters and sheltered coves. Sharks and manta rays patrolled the sandbars. Offshore, boiling schools of sardines darkened the sea. Bottled-nose dolphins and big-eyed tunas herded the tiny fish to the surface where royal terns and gannets dive-bombed them. Right whales gorged on the sardines. They flew over fishing dhows using runaround nets to encircle the migrating fish. The fishermen waved as they flew overhead.

Rigby blurted, "Wish Helen could have seen this."

Lily counterfeited a humorless smile.

Again the sightseeing novelty wore off. Everyone slept except Rigby, the designated pilot. His daydreaming drifted back forty years when he first met Lily. When the memory became erotic, he erased it and concentrated on the flight instruments.

Dark clouds began building offshore. The air became unstable. The amphibian bounced and bucked enough from the turbulence to wakeup Penny. He scanned the horizon and yawned.

A thunderstorm yielding slanted rain got his attention. He pointed at a jagged bolt of white lightning saying, "I don't like the looks of that. We better layover at Pemba. Think you can manage the landing, Croxford?"

"I'm not sure."

"Of course, you can. I'll walk you through it. C'mon now, relax."

Penny walked Rigby through the landing. Rigby's effort wasn't perfect, but as Penny said, "Not a smashing success, but at least you didn't collapse the landing gear. The good news... we survived it."

The hotel at Pemba was a step-up from their last hotel. After checking in, Penny took Rigby aside. "I need to speak to you in private." Rigby followed Penny up to his room. Penny spread an aeronautical chart on the floor. Lost in thought, he tapped his teeth with a pencil dimpled from nervous chewing. He looked like he was working a crossword puzzle.

"Jesus, Penny, you look serious."

"Indeed. Something's come up. Care for a whiskey?" Penny poured four inches of Jamison's into two water glasses and handed one to Rigby. "Here's mud in your eye."

They clicked glasses. Rigby returned the toast. "Bottoms up."

"I'm worried," Penny said

"Worried about what?" Rigby asked.

Penny grew introspective. He took off his glasses. After vigorously polishing a lens he held them up to the light. He squinted at Rigby. "What happens if I die?"

"What's that suppose to mean. Are you always this depressing when you drink?"

Penny appeared tipsy. "There's a good possibility I won't be making the return trip home. Now, I've got a call in for Otto. Can't seem to raise him. Bloody telephones in this country are useless. I'm afraid you're going to end up on your own, old boy. I've penciled the course lines with the fuel stops circled and the distances and I've calculated the fuel burn. God, I hate leaving you in this fix."

"Leaving? Who said anything about leaving?"

"Before you say anything, I have the utmost confidence in your piloting abilities. Otto was a good teacher. I know you have questions."

Rigby raised his eyebrows. "You're damn right I've got questions. What brought this on?

"What I'm trying to say is simple enough. The long and short of it is... I'm dying," Penny announced matter-of-factly.

"After lighting a cigarette, Rigby spoke through a lungful of smoke, "We're all dying."

"No, I mean I really am dying. Never expected to live this long. Suspect nobody does. Horrible watching your family and friends die. The thing I hate most about dying is the unanswered curiosities. Sorry, God knows I'm rambling a bit."

"I can't believe this. All of a sudden, out of the blue, you're dying? This is crazy talk."

"Listen to me. I spent sixty years flying wounded soldiers to hospitals in so many wars, I've lost track. I know dying when I see it. The blue lips and the shortness of breath, not to mention my tricky heart rate." Penny made his point by thumping his chest.

"No ifs, ands, or buts, I'm at the end of my rope. Actually, I've known my death was imminent for some time. Thought I could cheat the grim reaper one more time. Get in one last adventure. Sadly, I miscalculated." Penny lowered his eyes. "To tell you the truth, I always thought I'd die in an airplane. I'm afraid my candle is about to get snuffed."

Rigby looked frazzled. "I'm speechless."

After fortifying himself with a long gulp of scotch, Penny said, "Alright, for argument's sake, let's say Lily's daughter and her ex-husband are already dead. She needs closure. I'll carry on like nothing's wrong for as long as God allows."

"What about getting you into a hospital?"

"Die with tubes stuck in my arms. Breathing on a respirator. No thank you. Bear in mind what the English poet, Thomas, wrote." Penny raised his glass. "'Don't go gentle into that good night. Old age should burn and rave at the close of day. Rage, rage against the dying of the light.' Can't recall the rest of it. Anyway, you get the message. I hate giving up the race, but I've had a great run. It's time to hang up the old flying goggles, as they say."

Penny refilled their glasses. Slowly, Rigby disbelieving stare dissolved. "Penny, were you ever married?"

"Wasn't everyone? Twice. In a way, I killed them by exposing them to Africa. Pestilence, civil wars, famines and wild animals. Africa has it all. I've been searching for a cure for my addiction with Africa my whole life. Obviously, I haven't been successful. Sadly, both my wives paid the ultimate price. God bless their souls and curse mine. I was a frightful husband. Drank too much from the cup and I had too many one-night stands. Away from of home so much, I reckon. Lots of regrets, I'm afraid."

More silence. Finally, Rigby asked, "What about kids?"

Penny took a big swig of Scotch and grimaced when it hit bottom. "One... she died from black-water fever." Tears filled his good eye. He waved off any clarification and wiped the eye. "Your Helen was a gem. You're a lucky man. I'm sure you don't see it that way. I mean because of what happened to Helen. I'm worried about you, Croxford."

"Glad somebody is. I'll be all right. One day at a time, as they say."

"Mortality has a seat at every man's table. May I offer you a serious thought from someone who's never been serious about anything in his entire life? Just remember one thing, you're not God."

"Now you sound like my daughter. Where's this going?"

"Why not give Lily a chance. That's all I'm saying. By the way, for some unknown reason, she fancies you. Thinks you hung the moon. Obviously, the poor girl's delusional."

"Lily fancies who I was forty years ago. Time changes everything, especially people."

"Listen to *me* giving *you* advice," Penny said. "Don't pay any attention to me. I talk too much when I'm pissed. I was an awful husband."

"I doubt you were that bad," Rigby said.

"Wish I could make amends."

They were silent for a while, each lost in their private thoughts tainted by whiskey. Penny walked over to the window and stood there with his fingers interlaced behind his back.

The afternoon had produced a light drizzle. He stared absentmindedly at the droplets sliding down the window. Without turning he slurred, "I need to get something off my chest. Will you hear my confession, Padre?"

Also feeling the effects, Rigby muttered, "Proceed, my son."

The memory came back to Penny, rising up from the dark depths of his past. "It's about what happened to the president of Mozambique, Samora Machel in 1986.

"If memory serves, Machel died in an airplane accident."

"Accident? I know what *really* happened." Penny confessed his role in the plot to assassinate Mozambique's first black president. Returning from a conference in Zambia, Machel's private aircraft was scheduled to land on a foggy night in Maputo, Mozambique, but the pilot locked onto a decoyed navigational beacon and slammed into a hillside in neighboring South Africa. "God forgive me, thirty-three people died that night, including the president."

"That rumor has been around for years. How can you be so certain?" Rigby asked.

"Because I helped construct the phony beacon. Never told us why we were building it."

Rigby leaned forward. "Why did you keep this a secret?"

Penny wolfed down more Scotch. "For Queen and country, I suppose."

"No sense doing a post-mortem. It's water under the bridge," Rigby said.

"Not for me it isn't. Basically, I'm a coward. Looking back, I believe the Russians were responsible. Couldn't take them lightly,"

Penny admitted with a disarmingly self-depreciating smile.

"You're no coward. You might have saved the world from another African despot."

"Or robbed the world of another Mandela. If you remember, Machel's widow married Nelson Mandela."

"A martyr is always bigger in death than he was in life."

Rigby's face had hardened. "I did terrible things in the name of patriotism... we all did. War turns men into monsters and as such we do despicable things to each other."

Penny pontificated on the deteriorating state of warfare. "I've seen a lot in almost ninety years. I was always too lazy to work for a living and too damn jumpy to steal. Flying has been my life. What the hell happened to proper wars?" He cited victories at Waterloo when Wellington defeated Napoleon and Monty beating Rommel at El Alamein. He even referred to Cornwallis's defeat at Yorktown. His diatribe ended on the use of unmanned drones and incendiary explosive devices and commandeering child soldiers.

"Why, there's no bloody line in sand." He went on to say, "You can't distinguish good from evil. And another thing, what's so grand about death in battle without glory?" His speech left him breathless. He stared off into space and added, "Albert Einstein said the next world war will be fought with stones."

Rigby laughed humorlessly. "I'll say one thing—you certainly know how to brighten a room."

Penny said, "Bloody grim stuff, Croxford."

"Something beyond bloody grim," Rigby added drunkenly. "In vino veritas—in wine there is truth."

"Well put." Penny hiccupped. "God, I love Africa. Here's to her." He raised his glass as a toast. "From one Afro-junkie to another."

"I'm not sure Africa still loves us," Rigby cautioned, clicking glasses.

Penny's voice cracked emotionally. "Maybe so. I just needed to clear the deck, before, you know...."

Rigby stood up. "Penny, you're the finest man I've ever known. Now for God's sake, get some sleep."

Penny grabbed Rigby's hand. "Thanks awfully. If I could have had a son, I wish he could have been you, dear boy."

"It would have been my pleasure, sir."

"Goodnight."

Penny waited for the door to close. He placed a nitroglycerin tablet underneath his tongue. His thoughts focused on Rigby and Rhodesian Bush War. He was flying a Dakota jump plane on a tar-black night. *He had been partying when the emergency call came though. Rigby and five other jumpers had been recruited to parachute into a hot zone. The mission was to rescue survivors of an ambush. It was a low altitude deployment. The terrain was hilly. He remembered switching on the green light just as we crested over a hill. The next hill appeared out of nowhere. The first jumper was killed instantly. The second parachutist broke his back. Rigby, the third jumper was uninjured, even though he the hit ground seconds after leaving the airplane. At the military inquiry, Rigby refused to give evidence against him. The drinking issue never came up. They never discussed the incident again.*

Mercifully, Penny passed out.

17

The morning found Penny in much better spirits. He rounded up everyone and had them at the airport before the sun reddened the sky over the Indian Ocean. Rigby, Lily and Jed were still half-asleep. Penny climbed up into his amphibian's cockpit with the spryness of a much younger man. It was a miraculous recovery.

He taxied to the end of the runway. "Good God, Rigby, you look like death warmed over. Those who hoot with the owls at night shall not soar with eagles in the morning. Fasten your seatbelt, Croxford. Let's get cracking. We're off to Tanzania. And remember, air sickness will not be tolerated."

Rigby pressed his temples and yelled over the engine noise. "Remind me never to drink with you again, Penny. Seems like I've done-this-been-there before with you."

"Oh, one bit of history I forgot to mention last night. Did you know that a descendant of the Jamison family was with Henry Stanley when he surveyed the Congo Basin for King Leopold of Belgium in 1876? More of a land grab, actually."

"You mean the Jamison Scotch people?"

"Precisely. Seems our young James Jamison bought a slave girl and presented her to some very disagreeable natives. Wanted to document a barbecue, I reckon."

Rigby grimaced. "Thanks for the uplifting history lesson."

Penny continued, "Don't mention it. Stanley vowed to kill Jamison, but he died from malaria before Henry could shoot the bastard. Dreadful, the way revisionists muck things up."

Rigby burped painfully. "God, I feel awful."

"You're an amateur, Croxford."

The Cessna-185 lifted off and headed north. During the night, rain had cleansed the air of haze. The skyline and ocean were joined together in vivid shades of electric blue and green. The beach was blanketed in patches of orange seaweed. An occasional fishing dhow dotted the horizon. They flew over the palatial remnants of Persian and Omani settlements and deteriorated ancient mosques dating back to the twelfth century. He circled over Kilwa, a stopover for the slave caravans headed north. The crumbling ruins had been invaded by the jungle and unrelenting ocean tides.

"What happened to these people?" Lily shouted.

Penny replied, "Devoured by Muzimba cannibals, actually. Unpleasant chaps with rather odd culinary habits. Am I right, Croxford?"

Rigby said, "You are indeed. Another one of Africa's nasty secrets revealed."

"You must be kidding?" said Lily.

"Hardly. Human testicles were considered a delicacy by the Muzimba."

"Ouch!" Rigby yelled.

"Bon appétit," said Penny and added cheerfully, "Enjoy."

Everyone laughed, except Jed. The reality was too close to home. He pretended to be asleep. Penny turned back on course.

The next two hours were uneventful.

One hundred miles south of the Dar es Salaam Airport in Tanzania, the Cessna started to bank slowly offshore. They thought Penny had seen something of interest, but then the climbing turn steepened. At ninety degrees, the stall indicator buzzed a warning. The Cessna shuttered momentarily, and then it fell out of the sky. The wingover stall sent them spinning earthward. The windshield view was nothing but green water. Lily screamed. Jed grabbed Penny. As Rigby seized the yoke his memory went into overdrive. He remembered Otto saying, resist the temptation to jerk. Push and level the wings. When all fails, let go of the controls. She'll either right herself or the next thing you'll hear will be a very loud bang. He pushed the rudder peddle contrary to the spin and gently shoved the yoke forward. The old Cessna grudgingly complied. They were still falling, but the spinning had stopped. Rigby eased back on the yoke. They were level again at three hundred feet.

Lily screamed, "That wasn't funny, Colonel Pennington. Damn you to hell!"

Rigby glanced over at Penny. His head was slumped forward. His arms dangled by his sides. Penny's face, drained of color was as ashen as a winter sky. Rigby touched his neck hoping for a pulse. He turned Penny's chin sideways. The good eye was open and sightless. Rigby looked back at Lily and shook his head. Lily shivered and pressed her hand over her mouth. Jed crossed himself. Rigby suffered a moment of uncontrolled panic, but he slowed down his breathing and calmed himself. He started a slow steady climb and turned toward Dar es Salaam. He was trying desperately to think ahead. Thoughts of the landing made his queasy.

Ten miles out, Rigby radioed the airport. "Airport at Dar es Salaam, we have an emergency. Can you read me?"

"The aircraft calling, say call sign and aircraft type?" Unable to understand the command, Rigby glanced at Lily. She shook her head.

"The pilot is deceased—I repeat, the pilot is deceased. We need to land immediately," Rigby announced using the radio.

"Understand someone onboard is ill."

"Not diseased. I said deceased, as in dead. The pilot is dead."

"The pilot's name is Fred?"

This can't be happening, Rigby thought. "Jed, what's the Swahili word for stupid?"

"*Kijinga*," Jed answered.

"Look, *kijinga*, we're landing. End of story."

"To the aircraft calling, you are denied permission to land. Repeat, you are not cleared for landing. Return to your departure airport. We do not have quarantine facilities."

"I need to speak to someone who understands English."

Almost immediately, a substitute controller came on the air. Rigby told the replacement that a man onboard had died. In the confusion, he neglected to say it was the pilot. The controller asked for more details, but Rigby was too nervous to respond. They conversed in a combination of carefully enunciated Swahili and broken English. The minutes grew longer. "Where's the bloody airport," he said aloud. He felt the involuntary retraction of his testicles.

A few more minutes lapsed. At last, Jed spotted the airport beacon. The stuttering controller gave Rigby the first of three vectors to a final approach for landing on runway-270. The orange sun blinded him as he turned onto a final approach. He shaded his eyes. The runway approach lights flashing in sequence came into view. He'd rehearsed the landing a dozen times in the last thirty minutes. He flexed his shoulders and worked the stiffness out of his hands. Steady now... you can do this, he reassured himself. The runway was dead ahead. He retarded the throttle and lowered the landing gear. I've missed something, damn it, he thought. But what? He repeated the landing check-list out loud. You idiot, you forgot the flaps. He pulled the flap lever up to 20 degrees. Penny said to keep her at 80 knots. Suddenly, the airspeed bled down to 60 knots and then raced up to 90 knots. The engine groaned a warning. He retarded the throttle and pushed the yoke forward. The airplane's nose wandered left of the center line. They were headed straight for an ancient DC-3 abandoned by the side of the runaway. He jammed the right rudder pedal until the Cessna's nose centered. The ground came up fast. Everything outside passed by in a blur. He crossed over the threshold, eased back the yoke and closed his eyes. It was a perfect touchdown. He exhaled for the first time in what seemed like an eternity. Lily threw her arms around his neck and kissed him. Jed cheered and patted him on the back. He glanced over at Penny and breathed a loud sigh of relief.

Rigby taxied the Cessna to the ramp, shut down the engine and just sat there staring straight ahead. He couldn't speak. Finally, he undid Penny's seatbelt and gently pushed his head back against the headrest. He closed Penny's working eyelid.

A wave of sadness washed over him. Penny had been exceptional at cheating death. He had witnessed Africa's triumphs and her failures, and now he was gone.

I'm blessed for having known you, he thought. And then he said aloud, "I'm gonna miss you, old chap."

Within seconds they were surrounded by airport emergency vehicles, two police cars and a pickup truck, all had lights flashing. The policemen removed Penny's body from the airplane and placed him in the back of the pickup truck. They covered his corpse with a dirty green canvas tarpaulin.

Lily and Jed took a taxicab to their hotel. Rigby stayed behind to handle the Criminal Investigation Department's inquiry and to make the burial arrangements. The post-mortem inquisition lasted for three hours.

Later, from the privacy of his hotel room, Rigby found the following note stuffed in Penny's duffel bag:

Dear Rigby,

If you are reading this, my prediction was spot-on. No mourning for me, thank you. I had a great life. I'm ready to meet my maker. I hereby appoint you as my trustee. Sorry about that. I have no living heirs. I bequeath my airplane and my house in Victoria Falls to the Save the Rhino Foundation. I leave my guns and my book collection to you and Otto Bern. You will find my life's savings in the first edition of Churchill's, The Last Lion. Sorry it isn't more. Please use the money for a cocktail party. I meant what I said about wishing you were my son.

All the best and God's speed.

Your friend and admirer,

Harold Pennington

18

Terrance Cassidy and Lily Rosen had arrived in Tanzania at approximately the same time. The manhunt for David Levy converged in Dar es Salaam. Their motivations were poles apart. Cassidy's interest was the reward money. Lily's incentive was more complicated.

For Rigby, Penny's death was devastating. For Lily, it was an inconsequential setback. She knocked on Rigby's hotel-room door. As soon as she entered she noticed the gin bottle sitting on his night stand. Both Jed and Rigby looked out of sorts. Jed excused himself and left the room. She studied him with aggravation weeping out of her pores.

"So, where do we go from here?" Lily asked Rigby impatiently.

"Go? I'm not going anywhere. Care for a drink?" His words ran together.

Her face cast an enraged mould. "You're shitfaced," she snapped. She looked like she could barely control her anger. "Your escape from reality was always booze."

His eyes were unfocused. "Yes, yes. I'm pissed... so what if I am. I've got news for you—I aim to get much drunker."

"Doesn't Sarah mean anything to you? Look, I'm sorry your friend died. But I haven't got time to wallow with you in self-pity. How can you live with yourself?"

"Lily, to tell you the truth, I haven't lived with myself since my wife died."

She stared at him for a long second. "Fine. I'll find her without your help." Her tirade was heart-piercing enough to leave him speechless. She stormed out of his room and slammed the door behind her.

"Lily, wait," he shouted.

She didn't stop or answer.

Lily started her search at the Dar es Salaam's port district. Her queries led her to an agent in the Tanzanian Customs and Immigration Office. The Black Cygnet had cleared customs two months earlier. By chance, her driver vaguely remembered ferrying the Cygnet's crew members around town. Fifty Euros improved his memory. He said he was sure the Black Cygnet was still docked someplace in Dar es Salaam.

Her next stop was the harbormaster's office. She played the helpless woman routine to the hilt. It worked like a charm. The harbormaster not only gave her the shipyard's address where the Black Cygnet was moored, he walked her outside and gave the directions to her driver in Swahili.

She arrived at the shipyard just as the sun was setting. She tried to dismiss her driver, but the man protested. "Madam, this place isn't safe for ladies. Let me accompany you."

"That won't be necessary," she insisted.

Reluctantly, he drove away.

Lily walked with so much confidence though the shipyard's main gate, the night watchman was shocked. He acknowledged her with a tilt of his hardhat. She nodded back glibly. The shipyard was deserted except for one man working under a dry-docked ship. His welding arcs provided flashbulbs of light. The Black Cygnet lay captive in her moorings between two Chinese fishing trawlers. Cabin lights indicated someone might be onboard. Lily took off her shoes and tiptoed down the gangway. The rear salon was empty. She heard sound coming from the forward cabin. The teak flooring was soundless. When she twisted the handle dog, the bulkhead door swung open and screeched a shrill warning. She froze for a full minute.

The companionway was pitch-black. The air was cool and dry. The television light coming from a porthole at the end of the passageway silhouetted a man sitting with his back to her. He was watching a pornographic video. Lily eased the door open. She stepped into the salon and knocked loudly. The man vaulted to his feet. "Fuck! You scared the shit out of me. Boarding a ship without permission can get a person killed." He looked her over from head to toe. "Who are you? What do you want?" He had tattoos on both forearms. His face ended in a spade-shaped goatee. He looked like a man better avoided.

"Are you the captain?" Lily asked ignoring his questions.

"That's right." He acted fidgety.

"Where's the owner?"

He muted the television. "He's dead. Where've you been living, on Mars? Lady, I'm gonna count to ten. If you're not off this boat,

I'm gonna throw you overboard."

"That would be extremely ambitious of you." Lily said taking the Walther out of her purse and calmly aiming it at the captain. A red laser dot danced on the man's forehead. "I'll ask you one more time. Think carefully, before you answer."

"Wait... wait just a minute. I'm repossessing this...this vessel for a European bank." The man eyed a Bombay chest against the wall. Lily walked over and pulled the top drawer open. She picked up a chrome-plated handgun and struck it into her pocket. "What's the name of the bank?"

"Excuse me?" His raspy voice sounded urgent.

"You heard me. What's the name of the bank?"

"I don't know what you're talking about."

"It's a very simple question, really." Her voice had taken on a serene quality.

"Wait. I think... it's the Royal Bank of Zurich or something like that," he stammered.

"How very odd. I live in Switzerland. I've never heard of the Royal Bank of Zurich. I suspect it doesn't exist." She retrieved a silencer from her purse and screwed it into the Walther's barrel.

He held up his hands. "Hold on. Take it easy, lady. That thing could go off."

"Oh, I'm sure it will," she whispered.

A crowd gathered at the shipyard's main entrance. Policemen held them at bay. Dockworkers dragged fire hoses and manned emergency water pumps. It was a feeble attempt to control the fire. Orange flames licked greedily at the Black Cygnet's furled sails. Her twin fiberglass masts melted like wax candles. Blackened glass potholes cracked before popping. Black billowing smoke blotted out the skyline. To protect the moored vessels, a tugboat towed the burning hulk away from the dock. The blaze illuminated the freighters and tankers lolling at anchor.

Rigby had followed Lily to the shipyard. He was prevented from entering the main gate by a security guard.

Terrance Cassidy's search had also led him to David Levy's yacht. Like Rigby, he was denied entrance to the boatyard. Both men were detained in the shipyard's main office. They struck up a conversation. When Cassidy mentioned David Levy, Rigby expressed his role in the search for Levy's stepdaughter. They were both released when the fire alarm sounded. Rigby and Cassidy stood together watching the Black Cygnet burn to her waterline.

Lily walked up behind Rigby and wrapped her arms around him. It startled him. "How'd you find me?" She asked him.

He prevaricated saying, "I saw the fire. Sorry about earlier."

"Forget it," she said. "I have."

He worked the crick out of his neck. "A bit over the top, wouldn't you say? Wow, talk about a twist of fate."

Her eyes darted. "What's that supposed to mean?"

"We fly halfway to Cairo. Puff, your ex's yacht disappears in a cloud of smoke. I don't know, Lily. The whole thing sounds fishy to me."

"We need to talk," she said slightly out of breath. "I know where they're holding Sarah."

"Oh, I almost forgot. Lily Rosen, this is.... What's your name again?"

"Cassidy," he said holding out his hand. "Terrance Cassidy."

Lily's polite smile dissolved. She appeared annoyed. It was obvious she didn't relish Cassidy's intrusion. She accepted his handshake. "Nice to meet you," she said disingenuously.

Rigby hooked her elbow. "Lily, you aren't gonna believe why Mr. Cassidy is here. Bloody coincidences are running amuck."

One thing was clear; Lily's agenda was a mystery. He was missing something hidden in a sea of deception.

19

Rigby, Lily, Jed and Terrance Cassidy met in Rigby's hotel room. Cassidy outlined his special assignment investigating David Levy. He included that he was the one responsible for exposing Levy in the first place. He described the botched arrest attempt and the subsequent chase to Brazil. When he mentioned Levy's illicit political donations, it raised Lily's eyebrows, which was not missed by Rigby. She asked, "I'm still confused. What are you doing here?"

Cassidy replied evasively, "I guess you could say to put an end to the rumors about David Levy. And there's a lot of embezzled money unaccounted for. What's your relationship to Levy?"

"Me? I was married to him a long time ago. Something I'd like to forget. The indiscretions of a misguided youth, I'm embarrassed to admit. Unfortunately, my daughter was with him when he was abducted." She acknowledged Rigby, who remained silent.

"I had no idea. I'm sorry," Cassidy said.

"What's important is that Sarah's alive and I now know where she's being held."

"How can you be sure?" Cassidy asked.

"Because the captain of the Black Cygnet told me so."

Cassidy's sudden appearance was a complication for Lily. Leaving him behind could jeopardize the rescue. She briefed him on the search for her daughter. "Mr. Cassidy, I'm privy to information you might find interesting. I'll get to that part in a second."

Rigby's spirits, low enough to begin with, sank to new depths. Penny's death overwhelmed him with a strange detachment. At this point, he didn't care enough to challenge Lily. Lily requested an aeronautical chart, which Rigby retrieved from Penny's duffel bag. She spread the map on the bed. "Find the Rufiji River for me," she demanded, indentifying the approximate location. "Good. Now, pinpoint these coordinates." She handed Rigby a slip of paper. "According to the Black Cygnet's captain, my ex leased a hunting concession on the edge of the Selous Reserve ten years ago." She pointed at a spot on the chart. "That's where we'll find Sarah. I'd bet my life on it." She turned to Cassidy. "And that's where you'll find your answers."

Rigby referred to the map scale. "The concession is a hundred kilometers from here, give or take." Rigby continued, "So, you're telling me the captain just volunteered this information?"

"More or less," Lily answered loosely. When she saw Rigby's suspicion, she explained that the Cygnet's captain was uncooperative at first. To make her point she brandished her Walther. "Let's just say…I assisted his memory. I witnessed prisoner interrogations when I was in the Israeli military. A cocked pistol to the temple can be very persuasive."

Lily flaunting her pistol shocked Cassidy. He looked horror-struck and stepped backwards.

"What about that fire?" Rigby's expression revealed a fresh wave of skepticism.

Lily claimed the captain was in the process of illegally selling the Black Cygnet on the black market. He panicked, setting the fire to cover his tracks. Again, her explanation sounded fanciful, but it was possible.

As Jed listened, he suspected Rigby was thinking with his heart.

Rigby said, "Lily, tell Mr. Cassidy about Penny and our little misadventure." Lily described what she referred to as, the flight from hell. After a long silence, Cassidy asked, "You mentioned a Cessna. What model?"

Lily looked at Rigby for clarification. "It's an amphibian."

"Probably a 185 or a 206." Cassidy indicated.

"So, I take it you're a pilot?" Rigby asked Cassidy.

"Air Force ROTC at the University of Kentucky. I logged one hundred hours. How much flying time do you have, Mr. Croxford? Cassidy asked.

"Solo?" Rigby asked thinking, he doesn't know it yet, but he's our new pilot.

"Yes, of course."

"One." Rigby answered.

"One thousand or one hundred?"

"Well, let me see, that would be one hour in total. But it was an absolutely brilliant effort. Am I right, Lily?"

Lily frowned. She addressed Rigby. "Speaking of pilots, did you talk to Otto Bern?"

Rigby said, "I spoke with Otto a few hours ago. He can't help us."

Lily looked distressed. "And why can't he help us, pray tell?"

"Otto's got an arrest-warrant problem. From his smuggling escapades, no doubt. He's prepared to meet us in Mozambique, but Tanzania is off limits. African prisons are dreadful affairs. Take it from someone who knows firsthand."

Cassidy's mouth fell open. He looked at Rigby and then at Lily.

"What about driving?" Lily inquired.

Rigby referred to the map again. "Even if we had a proper vehicle, which we don't, there aren't any decent roads. Flying is our best option. Flight time in the amphibian would be less than an hour."

"What we need is an *experienced* pilot," Lily quipped. "Yesterday's nightmare shortened my life."

They both stared at Cassidy. "Hey, I haven't flown in two years."

Rigby grinned. "They say it's like riding a bicycle."

"I gotta clear this with my boss," Cassidy mentioned.

"By the way, who *do* you work for?" Lily asked.

Cassidy's face drew a blank stare as he pondered her question. "You *could* say I work for the American government." He scrutinized the map and looked at Rigby. "I can't find the frigging airfield. How're we gonna land?"

Rigby used his finger to trace the Rufiji River on the map. "What'd you expect, Jan Smuts International? Most hunting concessions have private grass-strips. If not, we can always land on the water."

"I've never even flown *in* a seaplane, let alone *pilot* one," Cassidy pointed out.

Rigby's smile widened. "Piece of cake. I'm sure together we can manage it."

"How many water landings have you made, Mr. Croxford?" Cassidy inquired.

Rigby faked racking his memory by scratching his head. "Well, let me see now. One and it wasn't solo."

"Penny for thoughts, Miss Rosen." Cassidy said.

She put her hand on Rigby's shoulder. "You don't wanna know. His daughter claims he's been vaccinated against the most basic human frailties, like fear and self-doubt." Lily pointed out, "The men who executed my ex-husband are violent thugs. Things could get messy. We have to do this. You don't, Mr. Cassidy."

Envisioning the reward money again, Cassidy said, "You need a pilot and I need answers. I'm in." Greed had trumped his trepidation.

"You get us there, I'll do the rest. Your job ends with helping me with the flying. Understood?" Rigby paused, daring Cassidy to disagree.

Cassidy nodded. "No argument from me on that point."

"Good. Whoever they are, they're about to meet our secret weapon." Rigby grinned looking at Jed.

Jed uttered a string of Shona curse words internally as he thought about more flying.

JAMES GARDNER

20

Rigby voiced his earlier concerns about the Tanzanian authorities allowing them to leave the country. Their international flight plan listed Pemba, Mozambique as the destination with Lindi as an alternative. Surprisingly, their passports were stamped by the customs and immigration agents without hesitation. The airport security guards even escorted them to the Cessna. The idea that someone wanted them out of Tanzania crossed Rigby's mind.

Cassidy and Rigby spent an hour preflighting the Cessna and another fifteen minutes going over the instruments. Money was front and center in Cassidy's mind when he announced, "I guess I'm ready, if you are?" He wiped his sweaty palms on his pants.

Rigby remarked, "Remind me to tell you about the time I crash-landed in the Sudan."

"Did you have to mention that damn crash again? I must be crazy," Lily said as she climbed up into the backseat. Jed crossed himself and fastened his seatbelt.

The Cessna's wings wobbled as they lifted off. At first, Cassidy didn't have command of the amphibian, but the morning air was smooth and the winds were light.

After a few turns, he got a better feel for the airplane. He flew south along the coastline for thirty minutes. When they passed west of Bwejuu Island, he turned inland and followed the Rufiji River.

As Rigby stared down at the river, he envisioned Henry Stanley's transcontinental march across Africa one hundred and fifty years ago. Stanley's first journey to find Dr. David Livingston was remarkable. The explorer's two-and-half year expedition from Zanzibar to the Congo was Herculean. Stanley with three hundred and fifty men and his guide, the infamous Swahili-Arabic slave and ivory trader, Tippu Tip, at his side waged battles against disease, famine and hostile natives. Stanley and Livingston were cut from different swaths of cloth. A spiritual soul, Doctor David Livingston was a healer of men. Henry Stanley may have been a cruel self-promoting egotist, but you had to admire his drive. He may have been short in stature, but he was long on testosterone, Rigby thought. He pondered his own legacy. I wonder how my family will remember me

Cassidy yelled over the engine's husky growl. "How far is it?"

Rigby checked the GPS and replied, "According to this, forty-two nautical miles."

"It all looks the same," Cassidy observed noting the bleak khaki-colored landscape passing beneath them. Rigby handed the aeronautical chart to Jed. "Your eyes are better than mine. See if you can locate the encampment."

After flying to the designated spot on the chart, Cassidy made ever widening three hundred and sixty degree turns. They had been circling for an hour when Cassidy voiced his concern about conserving enough fuel to reach Pemba. Just when their search seemed doomed to failure, something caught Jed's eye.

He asked Cassidy to fly lower over an island in the middle of the river. A closer look revealed a compound camouflaged under a thicket of umbrella acacias. Two drab green Land Rovers were parked inside the perimeter fencing. Cassidy noted a clearing a few kilometers from the campsite. The X in middle of a circle indicated a landing pad for a helicopter.

Rigby said to Jed. "You've got the eyes of an eagle. Not bad for an old man."

Jed beamed. When he thought about landing on the river his smile melted into a frown.

"Now, let's find a safe place to land," Cassidy said.

Lily yelled into Cassidy's ear. "The operative word is safe, Mr. Cassidy."

Cassidy suffered a last minute panic attack. "I'm gonna need your help landing this thing, Mr. Croxford." They flew away from the island. The muddied river lined by overhanging trees made sharp twists and bends, but finally it straightened out. "Think that stretch is long enough?" he asked Croxford.

"Looks good to me," Croxford replied.

"Okay, here we go." Cassidy flew downwind longer than normal. He planned on making an extended final approach. This would give him ample time to abort the landing if something went wrong. Rigby searched for dislodged trees or exposed boulders, but the touchdown spot looked clear of obstacles. Cassidy banked around one hundred and eighty degrees and pulled in twenty degrees of flaps. "Something doesn't suit you, for God's sake, speak up, Mr. Croxford."

"You're doing great," Rigby yelled cinching up his seatbelt. Lily braced herself. Jed closed his eyes.

Rigby called out the altitude and airspeed changes. "One hundred feet and eighty knots... fifty feet and seventy-five on the airspeed ... you're too flat." Rigby grabbed the yoke and pitched up. He made a last second correction to miss what looked like partially submerged boulders. The amphibian skipped like a flat-stone hurled against a pond, but quickly fell off the step and settled into the river. Rigby dropped the rudder handle and water-taxied until the floats bumped up against the riverbank. He pulled the mixture knob. The Cessna coughed twice and quit. Cassidy extended his trembling hands with the palms down. "Wow! Where'd those boulders come from? Can't believe we made it."

"Those weren't boulders, they were bloody hippos," Rigby said. "Antisocial buggers, of sorts. Hitting a three-thousand kilogram hippo would have ruined our day."

Lily touched Cassidy's shoulder saying, "Thanks for not killing us."

"Don't thank me—thank him. He landed it," he said acknowledging Rigby.

After Rigby and Jed spoke in Shona, Jed scrambled up the embankment and disappeared into the thick elephant grass. Rigby went to work unscrewing the hatch-covers on the floats. After he retrieved the rifles, he refastened the covers.

Minutes later, Jed reappeared. Rigby said, "According to Jed, this place is infested by lions."

Jed estimated the distance to the island campsite at four kilometers. Rigby ordered Lily and Cassidy to stay with the airplane while he and Jed searched for a shallow place to ford the river. As he explained, crocodiles are endemic in African rivers.

Swimming was not an option.

Lily wasn't having it. "You're not leaving me. I'm the only reason we made it this far."

"For God's sake, Lily, we're not out for a stroll in Hyde Park. We'll come back for you. You've got my word on it." Reluctantly, she accepted his order.

"Oh, one more thing, Lily, I need your red nightdress."

"What?" she asked. "By the way, it's a Chanel and it cost me a damn fortune." Saved it for what proved to be the nonevent of the century, she reflected bitterly.

He explained that Masai warriors wear red sarongs. The Masai have been hunting lions for centuries. In fact, killing a lion is a rite of passage for would-be warriors. "I've seen Masai cattle herders chase starving lions off a kill. Damn it, Lily, I need that nightgown."

Jed retrieved Lily's suitcase from the amphibian's luggage compartment. Lily cursed as she rummaged. She found it. Jed took off his shirt. Struggling into the nightgown he tore a sleeve. Lily sighed, shook her head and looked away. "Well, that's just great."

"I'd stay in the plane if I were you," Rigby suggested. "No telling what's out and about."

Rigby and Jed slung rifles over their shoulders and waded into the river papyrus reeds. Mosquitoes tormented them. The men ran up the riverbank cursing and swatting their arms and necks. They emerged under a canopy of whistling thorn trees. After reaching the crest of the shoreline, Jed found the tire tracks overlaid by pugmarks. Rigby asked, "How long ago?"

Stooping, Jed whispered, "The vehicle, yesterday. The lions, last night." Rigby motioned for Jed to take the point and lead the way. "You're sure about the time?"

Jed gave him a gap-toothed grin. "Only a real African can know these things."

As they walked they saw the river intermittently between the thorny trees. Jed sifted the animal sounds for danger. Shafts of sunlight cast moving shadows on the ground. Hornbills clinging to the tree trunks, cocked their heads listening for insects. Jed pointed at crocodiles slithering down the opposite riverbank. Their presence frightened troops of clucking guinea fowl. Baboons barked. Vervet monkeys gibbered. Hippos grunted. The cacophony masked the sound of a miniature drone hovering overhead.

They came upon the skeletal remains of animals scattered amongst the trees. The earthy smell of the river was overshadowed by the stench of putrefying flesh. Rigby breathed through his mouth and covered his nose with a handkerchief. Jed pointed at more lion tracks. They stopped dead in their tracks. A low guttural growl carried on the wind. Deep resonating snorts answered from the opposite direction. They were surrounded by lions. The men quickened their pace, but they didn't run. As they got closer to the island they found rotting animals suspended from tree limbs. Clouds of buzzing insects swarmed over the carcasses. Oozing maggots dripped to the ground beneath the glassy-eyed animals.

They marched until they could see the island. Jed discovered a cleared path to the river's edge. They discovered a small boat powered by an outboard motor held fast to a rickety wooden pier. They leaned their rifles against the dock. Rigby lit two cigarettes and handed one to Jed. "This place gives me the fucking willies."

Jed said, "Lions roar at night, not...." He hesitated cupping his ear. He thought he heard something, but then the wind shifted and there was only the alarm call of a go-away bird and the chuckle of water trickling over rocks.

Rigby was hand-cranking the outboard, when he heard, "Hold it right there!" An armed man dressed in camouflage stepped out from behind a tree. He was a large man with muscled arms and legs. He wore a wireless headset and mirrored sunglasses. Rigby and Jed raised their hands.

Rigby announced, "Thank God, you found us."

"You're trespassing on private land," the man shouted back.

Rigby said, "Sorry to intrude. Seems we've had a bit of a problem with our aircraft. We were hoping you might lend us a hand."

"Helping you ain't up to me. Can't believe you weren't attacked by the lions," the man said. I must be overfeeding them, he thought. He raised a finger indicating an incoming call. He conversed in a hushed secretive tone.

Rigby spoke to Jed in Shona, "Where'd he come from? Seems the real African has lost his edge. Old age, no doubt."

Jed shrugged.

21

A security guard controlling a drone studied live video feeds. Strategically placed cameras provided him with bird's-eye views of the island including the docking area on the other side of the river. Scanning the monitors, he spoke into his mouthpiece. "After you deliver them, pick up the other two at the seaplane. Did you copy that?"

"Roger." He faced Jed. "Hey, you in the red dress, sit down before you capsize us."

"Better do as he says," said Rigby.

Jed bristled but he complied.

Rigby and Jed had worked in exclusive hunting camps, but this one was over the top. No expense had been spared. A generator humming in the background supplied electricity. A smartly dressed servant scurried between the out buildings. The grounds were manicured. The two Land Rovers parked under an umbrella acacia looked new. Expensive linen fluttered on a clothesline. Classical music blared from hidden loudspeakers.

The man who met them at the landing was a tall muscular South African. He also wore mirrored sunglasses. He nodded at the crocodiles swimming around the dock.

"As you might have guessed, we feed them. Our helicopter pilot doubles as the camp's mechanic. He's due back tomorrow morning. Looks like you'll be spending the night."

They were shown to a chalet. The accommodations were luxurious. Rigby noticed there were no locks on the windows or the front door. The lions and the crocs are all the locks they need, he thought.

"Why don't you get settled in," said the security guard. There's not a lot to see, but you're free to roam the island. The main building is off-limits. Like I said before, stay clear of the river unless you have a death wish."

Rigby and Jed heard the watery burbling of an outboard engine. A few minutes later, Lily and Cassidy entered the chalet. Lily seemed wired. Rigby grabbed her arm roughly saying, "Okay, now what? We damn-neared killed ourselves getting you here. Not to mention what happened to Penny. Tell me this wasn't a waste of time."

Lily turned to Jed and Cassidy. "Can you give us a minute?" She waited until they were alone, then she said, "I never intended for this. I'd do anything for you. You have to know that."

"What I know, Lily, is that you haven't been straight with me."

Instead of answering she gave him a noncommittal stare.

"Let's start at the beginning? Who are you, I mean really?" he said.

"I'm anyone you want me to be. Or rather I can become that person. I can't replace Helen, but given time, I know I can make you happy."

"C'mon, Lily, first things first, have you told me the truth about anything?"

"You want the truth. I've never stopped loving you. There, you have the truth."

"I'm betting you were never married to David Levy. Tell me I'm wrong."

The absence of her response confirmed his allegation. "What are we doing here? There is no Sarah Rosen, is there? That lookalike photograph was a nice touch."

Lily shook her head. "I lied to protect you. Things are not what they seem to be. When did you know or rather what gave me away?"

"From the first time we met. Things didn't add up. And for one thing, your Walther's threaded for a silencer—hardly the preferred weapon for a novice. You pinched my daughter's note, didn't you?"

"Smart girl, your daughter. If you knew, why didn't you say something?"

He thought for a long moment. "I guess I wanted to believe you so much, I ignored my intuition."

His admission gave her a ray of hope. "So, you *do* care for me."

"Of course, I care for you. This...this endeavor, for the use of a better term, has put people's lives at risk. For what purpose, I haven't a clue. God damn it, Lily, I need answers."

"Are you sure you can handle the truth? I told you I've done terrible things in my life. I'm afraid you'll be repulsed."

"Try me," he said.

Lily started at the beginning. After she completed her required stint in the military, she was recruited by an Israeli intelligence service. She worked undercover as a foreign operative for nine years. She glossed over her sacking, but Rigby guessed it was over an operation gone sour. She was currently employed by a shadow international security concern, which was a euphemism for a company engaged in black operations. She spoke calmly. "We're mostly ex-CIA, former KGB and a few Mossad recruits. I receive my assignments by mail."

"So, the medical company you told me about is a figment of your rather vivid imagination?"

"Well, yes."

"Lily, I'll say one thing, you are without a doubt, the most accomplished liar I've ever known. It was an Oscar-winning performance, by any measure."

"Hey, I wouldn't be so quick to judge. Some stones are better left unturned."

"Interesting. How would you describe your work?" he asked.

Lily looked agonized. She told him she played the roles of girlfriends or wives of wealthy executives. When he asked for specifics, she spoke about an oil company needing to send someone to Iraq to negotiate an equipment contract. Bodyguards would draw unwanted attention. Because there was a danger of being kidnapped, Lily provided security by pretending to be the man's wife or girlfriend. As she gained experience, the nature of her assignments changed. When she seemed reluctant to elaborate, Rigby pressed her for more details.

Lily's explanation was vague. She said people do terrible things. If the victims are unable to obtain justice and if they have the means, they seek out people with the skills to see that justice is done. Her generic description was met by an unbelieving stare.

Lily said, "Under the circumstances, this may sound a bit premature. I've been thinking about what we talked about on that first night in your hotel room. We could work together. Who knows, our arrangement might lead to something more permanent. You already know the basics. My services don't come cheap. I've got more than enough saved to take care of us for the rest of our lives. And we could get your daughter and her son out of Africa. I own a villa on the Amalfi Coast in Italy and an apartment in Geneva, Switzerland. Not bad venues, if you think about it."

When Lily recognized his surprise, she downplayed her proposal. "Sorry, I'm getting a little ahead of myself. It's just that I'm running out of time."

He looked askance at her, thinking, what changed you. You're not who I remember. What happened? One thing stood out. For Lily, guilt was an unknown emotion. "You mean we'd be contract killers?"

"I wouldn't put it that way."

"How *would* you put it?"

"Simply put, I consider myself an arbiter of justice."

"Not sure that works for me," he said, sensing it was pointless to challenge her.

"You get used to it. The first time is the hardest. After that, it gets easier."

"Lily, you're a hired assassin, for Christ's sake."

She shot him a frustrated glance. "You must have a lovely view from your lofty perch. Hey, I wouldn't point fingers, if I were you. You were a mercenary, not a missionary."

"Touché, Lily. In my defense, I always fought for the underdogs. Usually on the losing side, including the Rhodesian Bush War, I regret to admit."

"How puritanical of you," she blurted satirically. "Believe it or not, sometimes hideous people do hideous things to each other. I make sure the guilty don't go unpunished."

Rigby seemed distracted. "Sorry, I didn't catch that."

"It wasn't important. Okay, let me give you an example. Four volunteer nurses are working in a Palestinian refugee camp. They're kidnapped by a local militia. The leader of militia is the son of a wealthy well-connected Saudi Arabian businessman. The nurses are raped by this scumbag. He has all four women tortured and killed. The brokenhearted families petition the Saudi government for justice. Of course, their pleas are ignored. Frustrated, they turn to a person who connects with another person who contacts my company in a roundabout fashion.

The rapist-slash-murdering Arab has a weakness for prostitutes. He maintains two flats in Paris. One used by his family and friends. The other flat was designated for his extracurricular activities. On a business trip to Paris he telephones an escort service. But the call is intercepted. No need to continue. We both know the ending."

Rigby knew her hypothetical was real. There wasn't the slightest doubt, Lily killed the Arab. He shuddered inwardly and looked away.

"Now, do you really think the world will miss that piece of shit?" She asked. "I say good riddance. I did the world a favor."

He raised a placating hand. "Let's talk about David Levy?"

Before Lily could answer, the South African opened the front door. "The boss wants to meet you."

They emptied out and followed him single file to an isolated building. Lily, Rigby, Cassidy and Jed were escorted inside. The windows were shuttered. African masks and paintings adorned the walls. The room would have been totally dark had it not been for a reading lamp on a desk. The man sitting behind the desk with his back turned said, "Sit down. Make yourselves comfortable."

David Levy swiveled around in his chair. Without monthly Botox injections, his face bore a striking resemblance to an architectural gargoyle decorating a medieval castle. The lumps and voids looked like hornet stings. His eyes were lifeless. The pouch under his chin hung like an old man's scrotum. Levy interlocked his fingers and used his thumbs to support his chin. He examined the four photocopies of passports displayed on his desk. Who are these barbarians at my gate? Who sent them, he thought. The possibilities made his pulse rate quicken, but he kept his cool.

"I understand you've had airplane problems. I'm surprised our lion recordings didn't discourage you." Levy snuffed his runny nose, a nuisance from his cocaine addiction. His face looked like a grinning skull.

Rigby answered. "Yes, that's right, we were forced to land."

"Great liars usually incorporate small elements of truth in their lies. Let's start over, shall we?"

"Pardon me," Rigby said.

"To borrow a line from a great movie, you're errand boys sent by grocery clerks to collect a bill." Levey's altered face twisted in

[185]

defiance. He singled out Penny's photograph and directed his lamp on Cassidy's face. A faint light of recognition registered. "You're not Pennington. Don't I know you?"

"We've met before. My name's Cassidy."

"I knew there was something familiar about you. Now, I remember. So, the politicos in Washington sent a babysitter. I'm not surprised. Terrified I might spill the beans before the upcoming presidential election." He held up a folder. "This is my deliverance from purgatory. Millions funneled into the leading presidential candidate's foundation and other politicians, I might add. If I don't get what I want, there'll be hell to pay. As a lawyer, I can assure you and the greedy bastards who sent you—impeachment will be the least of their worries. People will go to prison." Levy patted the ledger. "It's all here in black and white. The foreign bank account numbers, everything."

The lack of greetings between Rosen and Levy said volumes. Rigby asked Levy, "Can I ask you a question?" Levy nodded. "Who was the man executed in the photograph?"

"Enhanced computer imaging. Before you ask, it wasn't my idea. What's your role in this nefarious affair, Mr. Croxford?" Levy asked referring to Rigby's photocopy.

"At this point, I'm not sure," Rigby replied nodding at Lily. "Better ask her."

"You've met my man in charge. I'm afraid what happens to you from this point going forward is up to him," Levy said.

Lily laid a pair of mirrored sunglasses on his desk. "Well, now, you see you've got a problem."

Levy looked befuddled. "Sorry, I'm not following you."

"He doesn't work for you anymore. He works for me."

Levy appeared unconvinced. "Oh, really. Since when?"

"Since I burned your yacht in Dar es Salaam. I negotiated better retirement plans for your employees."

Levy's defiance began to ebb. "So, what happens now?" The grinning skull was no longer grinning.

"That depends."

"On?"

Lily removed a revolver from her purse. "I want the Swiss and Cayman bank account numbers. And I want the money you stashed and the diamonds."

"And what do I get in return, Miss Rosen?"

Her voice was both composed and convincing. "Let's start with your continued breathing." She fondled the Walther like it was a religious relic.

"C'mon, you can't be serious?" The absence of a response dried his mouth. He licked his lips searching for moisture.

Whispering, Lily asked Rigby to take Jed and Cassidy to the boat and wait for her there. When Rigby objected, she protested. "Please, just do as I ask. I know what I'm doing." The men complied. After they were alone, Lily screwed the silencer into the barrel of her revolver. Levy's eyes grew so large; they looked like they might burst. He gasped like a landed catfish. Fear-sweat beaded his chin. "Can't we come to some type of an agreement? Whatever they're paying you, I'll double it."

Lily said nothing. She gave him a knowing smile.

"Okay, okay, you win. He moved the chair he was sitting on, rolled up a sisal area rug and opened a trapdoor. The hiding space contained two large satchels, some cigar boxes and a Hermes briefcase. Lily grabbed the briefcase and opened it. She laid her pistol on the desk as she scanned some papers. Levy eyed the handgun and edged closer. "It's all there, everything you wanted—including the bank statements with hundreds of millions. Look, just don't hurt me. That's all I ask."

Levy and Lily lunged for the pistol simultaneously, but he was a fraction of a second quicker. Without hesitation he aimed the Walther pointblank at her face and pulled the trigger three times. When it failed to discharge, he shook the weapon like it was defective and pulled the trigger three more times. Reality sunk in. Levy was so terrified his bladder voided. He exuded an acrid nasty smell.

Lily retrieved a chrome-plated pistol from her purse. She cocked the hammer. Her demeanor turned eerily calm.

Levy's voice cracked. "You don't have to do this. How about cutting me some slack? I mean c'mon, we're both Jewish—that ought to count for something."

Her answer was an ingratiating smile. His terror ebbed. He relaxed and lowered his eyes. She put her hand on his shoulder in a consoling motherly fashion. He placed his hand on top of hers. "I promise, you won't regret this," he stammered drily.

"I know," she said."

The bullet entered behind his right ear. Levy's body stiffened. He turned as limp as a spent middle-aged lover. His head hitting the wooden floor made a meaty thump. A steady rivulet of blood pulsated from the dark hole in his head. Only his eyes were alive.

He looked up at her, but in a split second his pupils dilated. Levy's bowels let go filling the air with yet another stench. Lily placed the pistol in his right hand.

As she exited the building, she ran straight into Rigby, who gasped, "We heard a shot!"

Instead of answering she pointed at Levy's body lying in a growing pool of blood. "Our friend ran out of options."

"Did he, now," Rigby said doubtfully, pushing her out of the way. Levy's eyes were open and unseeing. The room was permeated by a metallic blood smell. "Please don't insult my limited intelligence, Lily. We both know what happened."

Before he could speak again, Lily said, "There's something you need to hear. I can't lie to you." She glanced at Levy. "He wasn't the only one with a bull's-eye on his back. There's a price on your head as well. When I read the contract, I could hardly believe my eyes. What's the likelihood, after all these years? I would do anything or say anything to protect you. I'm guessing you've figured that out by now. If I didn't get you out of Zimbabwe, you'd be dead. End of story. I lied to save your life. Someone is willing to pay a great deal of money to have you silenced."

"Why should I believe you after you so blatantly lied to me?"

"Because not believing me will get you killed. A word to the wise, they'll find you. You can rest assured your contract is being shopped around as we speak. Perhaps you think you're tough enough to handle this on your own. It doesn't work like that. It could be someone dressed like a priest or maybe even a nun. And it will happen when you least expect it. Believe me—I know the routine. Let your guard down for a second and bang, someone will fire a small caliber bullet into your brain. It's nothing personal—it's just the nature of the beast."

"Go back a second. Who the hell did David Levy piss off?"

"He robbed investors of their life's savings. But in my opinion it's someone or a group protecting an American politician. Levy was a blackmailer. Double-crossing can be a slippery slope. There's a long list of people who wanted Levy put under."

"Lily, did you do it?" He nodded at Levy. "For once, just be honest with me."

"At this point, what difference does it make? That's not the answer you expected, but that's all I'm gonna say."

"Who fingered me?" Rigby asked.

"Normally, I don't get involved in the 'who' part. With you, I made an exception."

"It was Dkari Sibanda, wasn't it?"

Lily shook her head. She handed him a photograph saying, "His name's Zhang Wei."

Rigby said, "We call him Uncle Mao. Always figured he was lower on the totem pole. Guess I underestimated him."

"The contract originated in Hong Kong. He's just the go-between."

Rigby speculated that the president of Zimbabwe was approaching ninety. The Chinese couldn't afford to take a chance with an unknown successor. Sibanda might be a criminal, but he was their criminal. They needed to protect Sibanda at all costs. His rift with Sibanda was common knowledge. By eliminating him, the threat to Sibanda is contained. That reality formed a mental image.

JAMES GARDNER

"Wow, Sibanda as our next president—talk about a fucking disaster. I knew he wanted me dead. Now the Chinese are after me. Nice to know I've become so popular. If you were me, what would you do?"

She tossed him a lazy grin. "You mean besides moving to Italy with me?"

He returned her grin. "Yes, besides that."

"A strong offense always trumps a defense. If I were you I'd eliminate the threat. Nip it in the bud, so to speak."

"By eliminate, you mean exterminate?"

Lily said, "Your words not mine."

"What happens next?" Rigby asked.

She told him about Levy's foreign bank accounts and the list of bribed politicians. Lily held up the Hermes briefcase. "Levy's diamonds and cash are in here. "Once Cassidy delivers this, minus what I owe Levy's men, to an American Embassy, he's home free."

Rigby raised an eyebrow.

Lily said, "Hey, don't look at me in that tone of voice. I may be many things, but a thief isn't one of them. This goes back to the victims. We do have our ethical standards, sir."

"I apologize," he said.

"Apology accepted. Anyway, Levy's helicopter should be here within the hour. I'll take Cassidy with me. Are you sure you and Jed can handle the seaplane? Last chance—Italy's magical this time of year."

"Sounds tempting, but I've got my daughter to look after.

JAMES GARDNER

And like I said, Africa is my obsession. I plan on being buried here, hopefully not in the near future." Those words ended Lily's fantasy of reviving their love affair. When he saw her disappointment, a tiny stab of regret touched his heart. He wished he'd softened his rebuff, but it was too late. He changed courses. "Lily, why don't you give it up? Someday, your luck has got to run out."

"As crazy as this sounds, I'm addicted to the adrenalin rush. And it's the only thing I've ever been good at. You've got your obsession. I've got mine."

Lily pulled his head down and kissed him. She looked into his eyes and then she kissed him again, this time deeper and longer. "I'll think of you often, Rigby Croxford.

Take care of yourself. Anything happens to you, my dream dies with you. Not sure I could deal with that. You ever change your mind—this is where you can find me." She stuck a slip of a paper into his hand. Guess I'll see you when I see you."

They both knew the odds against them ever seeing each other again were long. "I'm sure we'll get together soon enough," he lied, trying to soften their parting. He walked away and then he turned back around and shouted, "Levy was left-handed, Lily. You might consider putting that weapon in his left hand."

"Nice try, Croxford. Levy is or rather was right-handed."

He waved to her. "Stay well, Lily."

She blew him a kiss.

Cassidy and Rigby shook hands. Cassidy said, "Think you can fly her without me?"

"I'll manage. Have a safe journey," Rigby said, climbing into the skiff. "There is something you can do for me."

"Just name it," Cassidy said.

"I know about my work with endangered wildlife. As an American, your support would be greatly appreciated."

"Consider it done," Cassidy said.

Rigby waved goodbye and yelled, "Cheers."

Cassidy watched them disappear around a bend in the river.

Jed and Rigby pushed and prodded the amphibian clear of the bulrushes. Jed climbed up into the co-pilot's seat. Rigby primed the engine and turned the key. The engine coughed and fired on the second crank. Rigby added flaps and turned downriver. The river, furrowed by the wind whipped the water into foam-crested waves.

"Ready to go home?" he yelled over to Jed. Jed nodded, interlocked his fingers in prayer and closed his eyes. The old Cessna responded without the extra two passengers like a flushed wood duck, but the waves caused it to porpoise. Rigby tried to liftoff, but the seaplane wasn't ready to fly. The straightaway in the river disappeared into a meandering turn. Towering sausage trees appeared up ahead. It was too late to abort. The floats banged loudly. The airframe shuttered. Spray engulfed them. Jed braced for impact.

"Fly, you old bitch, fly!" Rigby yelled in vain. They lifted off with twigs smacking the bottom of the floats. Instinctively, Rigby banked vertically to miss the trees. The seaplane brushed treetops as it struggled to climb above the muddied river.

Rigby waggled the Cessna's wings as he roared over the compound. He looked for Lily, but couldn't find her. She was already headed back to Dar es Salaam. Tentacles of white smoke poured out of the windows and the doors. She's covering her tracks, he thought.

With the blistering African sun at its zenith, Rigby turned south down the coastline for Pemba in Mozambique. Hopefully, Otto Bern was waiting there. Rigby knew an uncertain future was waiting for him in Zimbabwe. It was another obstacle he faced. But for now, getting back to Zimbabwe was the first order of business.

The afternoon heat formed sparse puffy clouds along the coastline. Those clouds gave rise to air turbulence. The old Cessna bumped and rolled like an experienced lover in bed. Rigby tried to climb over the clouds, but their rapid buildup prevented him. He flew between the clouds as best he could. Offshore thunderheads began to form. One storm yielded a waterspout; its tentacle churned up the ocean. He tried to engage Jed in conversation to calm him, but Jed was too nervous to respond. He groaned and grunted with every bounce.

"Pretend we're riding down a corrugated road in a vehicle."

Jed looked down out of the copilot's window. "It is not the bumps I fear—it's the distance to the ground that concerns me."

Rigby piled it on saying, "Why, you old geezer, you've lived long enough for three men."

"If my feet ever touch the earth again, I promise to get right with the Lord."

Rigby reminded him. "My friend, I've heard you make that promise many times."

"Yes, but this time I swear I mean it," Jed said crossing himself.

Rigby pushed on. The low-hanging clouds forced him to fly lower. It was only ten kilometers to the Pemba Airport. The problem was getting there before he ran out of fuel. He remembered Otto's saying, 'the first rule of bush flying is never lose sight of the bush.' Easier said than done, Rigby thought looking ahead into the mist.

Without warning, the clouds thickened until they were flying blind. The Cessna was tossed about like a toy airplane.

He wiped the sweat from his eyes and scanned the flight instruments. He remembered flying with Otto into a dust storm. Keep the wings level and the airspeed constant. A healthy respect for altitude is the key element, he heard Penny say.

The inclement weather only lasted for a few seconds, but seemed like forever. They burst out of the clouds. The amphibian was bathed in brilliant sunshine. Rigby patted Jed's shoulder and pointed at the Pemba Airport. Reluctantly, Jed opened his eyes.

Otto Bern was waiting for them at the airport. Otto came on the radio and talked Rigby down. Rigby's landing wasn't perfect, but it was improved. As Rigby taxied to the ramp, he thought about Penny. You were with me today, old boy.

The next morning they departed Pemba bound for Zimbabwe. Otto took over the piloting duties. Rigby and Jed slept for most of the flight. Otto opted for a direct route over Malawi. After one refueling stop ten hours later, they landed at the Victoria Falls Airport.

Otto remarked that the customs and emigration airport officers seemed overly interested in Rigby's travel itinerary. They guessed that Dkari Sibanda had already been notified about Rigby's reentry into Zimbabwe.

22

New York

By the time Terrance Cassidy's flight landed at JFK, David Levy's apparent suicide and his execution hoax were relegated to the back pages. Cassidy's attempts to contact the National Security Agency's lawyer, James Middleton, the man who sent him to Africa, were unsuccessful. David Levy was dead. He was no longer a political liability. Cassidy was given the persona-non- grata treatment. What Middleton hadn't counted on was Jackie Atkinson. He had wronged the man she was determined to marry, and for that there would be no clemency.

She put her accounting background to good use. As an auditor for the Security Exchange Commission she was privy to pertinent government files. Using Levy's list of guilty political participants as a guide, she traced money funneled into their campaign war chests as well as their personal accounts. The more she dug the more she uncovered. There seemed no end to the gluttonous feathering of their nests. In some cases, offshore dummy corporate entities were used as conduits to hide the ill-gotten profits. Millions electronically transmitted around the world were channeled into political super funds. The contributions far exceeded the maximum amounts permitted by law. It was a bonanza for the presidential candidates. Jackie had uncovered a pit of ravenous vipers.

They met in his one-room flat on the lower west side of Manhattan. Cassidy tossed her findings on a Murphy bed. "This is some serious shit. We could be in over our heads."

"And let them shaft you? No way. They can't hurt us," Jackie snapped.

"Tell that to David Levy."

She tapped her long fingernails on her teeth. "But you said Levy committed suicide?"

"At this point, I'm not so sure."

She walked over to the window and stared into the gloomy night. A winter storm had settled in over the city. The streets were dusted in a light snow. The blue light from a police cruiser cast flashing shadows on the buildings. She raised her finger. "Trust me—I know how to handle our friend, James Middleton."

"You're sure," he asked attempting a weak smile.

"He wants to play hardball. We'll play his game," she said. "Right now, I need something to settle my nerves."

"But, you're on the wagon."

"That's not what I had in mind."

"God, I missed you," he said opening his belt.

Jackie unbuttoned her blouse saying, "There's something I forgot to mention. You've been invited to a wedding in two weeks."

"Oh, who's getting married?" he asked.

"You are." Jackie braced herself for a quarrel. When she saw his reaction, she threw her arms around him.

"Terry Cassidy, we're gonna make a great team."

Cassidy pulled off his left shoe. He emptied a diamond the size of a man's thumb into the palm of his hand. He handed it to her saying, "I haven't had time to shop for a setting."

She held the perfect ten caret pink diamond up to the light. The prisms magnified sparkling reflections on her face. "These acrylics look so real. Something smaller would have been nice."

"Real? Two diamond cutters at Oppenheimer's think we should insure it for fifty thousand dollars."

Jackie cocked her head. "Where'd you get this? Wait...wait, don't tell me."

"A woman in Africa gave it to me as a wedding gift."

"What's her name?"

"Let's just say, it's better if you don't know."

Three days later, Jackie and Cassidy flew to Washington for a meeting with James Middleton.

They were ushered into his office. Middleton didn't offer to shake hands, but he did apologize for not accepting Cassidy's telephone calls. The bulging vein in his neck indicated suppressed irritation. Middleton fidgeted impatiently as Cassidy recalled his African experience. When Cassidy finished speaking, he said, "You did a great service for the country, Mr. Cassidy. Is there anything else?" He stood up indicating that as far as he was concerned there was no reason to continue the meeting.

Cassidy started to rise, but Jackie's arm prevented him.

She said, "Just one minute, sir. Let's discuss the reward money."

Middleton looked aggravated. "Frankly, this is outrageous." He waved the threatening email she'd sent him in one hand and banged on the table with the other. "Miss Atkinson, this could be construed as blackmail. Your boss at the SEC is a friend of mine." He shook his finger at Cassidy. "I'm surprised you're involved in this...this shakedown."

"Sir, you sent my fiancé on a bootless errand to Africa. You know it and I know it. You endangered his life. Before you say something you might regret, I suggest you look at this." She flipped the list of implicated politicians on his desk. Her audacity shocked him. Middleton snatched the document up and scanned it quickly. He got the feeling he wasn't going to like the answer to his next question. "What's this about?"

"A complete record of the money Levy doled out to politicos. Let me rephrase that, it's a who's-who list of guilty politicians on the take."

Middleton looked at the ceiling taking in the details of what she was saying. "Since when did accepting political donations become illegal?"

Atkinson replied. "Since the money was embezzled from investors, including charitable foundations, I might add. Since millions wound up in personal accounts."

Middleton studied the list more thoroughly this time. His Adam's apple rose and lingered there longer than normal. He looked at Cassidy. "You're saying you obtained this list from David Levy in Africa? How do I know it's real?"

"Oh, it's real," Cassidy assured him.

"You believe this is bona fide?" Middleton asked Atkinson holding up the list of surreptitious bank account numbers.

"Yes, every word of it," she reiterated.

Middleton recalled the conversation with his lawyer-friend at the DNC. He sat down heavily in a wingback chair. After a short wait, he uttered, "I need to make a telephone call." He got up and left the room.

Middleton dialed his private line. The lawyer for the DNC picked up. Middleton said, "He's in my office as we speak and he's got the Atkinson woman with him. I thought we were home free, now this. Seems our hired idiot wasn't idiotic enough. They've got the list of participants with the bank account numbers and the money transfers. Jesus, I almost puked. They want the finder's fee I promised. Tell me what you want me to do?"

The lawyer said the only option was to pay them. They needed to do this without alerting the trustee. When Middleton voiced his concern, the lawyer said, Never underestimate the power of the presidency. His departing words were: You take care of your end—I'll take care of mine.

As Jackie and Cassidy waited they conversed in the following series of scribbled notes on the same piece of paper:

Cassidy wrote: He looked like he was about to have a coronary.

Atkinson wrote: We got him where we want him.

Cassidy wrote: Don't forget the job he promised me.

Atkinson was about to write when Middleton opened the door. Middleton looked more acquiescent.

"What is it you want, Miss Atkinson?"

Jackie said, "Let's start with his remuneration, shall we?"

Middleton responded saying, "If it's legal, I don't see a problem."

Cassidy said, "Oh, it's legal. It's covered under the Whistleblowers Protection Act."

"Someone will contact you," Middleton said sounding exasperated. "I already gave him your contact number. Is there anything else?"

"About that position you promised him," Jackie said.

"I'll see what I can do." When he saw their cynicism, he said, "Look, I'll do my best. That's all I can promise." Middleton stood up again.

"There is one more sticking point," Atkinson mentioned.

"Now what?" Middleton asked impatiently.

Cassidy retrieved a typewritten summary from his briefcase, known as the Global Anti-poaching Bill. The media named it the Cecil Lion Bill. Bill H.R. 2494 prevented the importation of large animal trophies into the United States.

Middleton scanned the summary. "Sorry, you lost me. What's this got to do with me?"

Cassidy reiterated Rigby Croxford's plea to save Africa's endangered animals. He concluded by suggesting possible tariffs if Viet Nam and China continued to import rhino horn and ivory.

"With all due respect, starting trade wars over animal parts is preposterous."

The wildlife conservationists are gonna be very disappointed, Cassidy thought.

As they got up to leave, Jackie added a parting shot, "So what happens now?"

"Nothing happens until you both sign nondisclosure agreements. This country doesn't need another political witch-hunt."

"We figured as much. What will you do with that?" She pointed at the list of politicians.

"Turn it over to the Department of Justice," Middleton prevaricated.

Atkinson asked, "And then what happens?"

"I'm not sure. Maybe nothing happens."

"But why?"

"If the corruption is as invasive as you claim, it's too disruptive. A presidential candidate might be implicated. If some congressmen got caught with their hands in the cookie jar, the country could get over it. Your allegation, real or imagined, could damage the public's trust."

"Trust? The approval rating for Congress is zilch," Atkinson said.

Middleton's hazel eyes enlarged behind his thick glasses. "Our democracy isn't perfect, but what government is? Would you consider moving to say, Africa?"

Cassidy shook his head.

"I didn't think so. I appeal to you as patriots. Let us clean our house from within."

"About the job you promised my fiancé. We'll get back to you on that."

Middleton grimaced like he had indigestion. "I understand."

23

Zimbabwe

The first incident occurred soon after Rigby Croxford reentered Zimbabwe. By putting his anti-poaching activism on hold and resuming his role as a photographic safari guide, he hoped Dkari Sibanda would drop his guard. When the right opportunity arose, Rigby would make his move.

Lily Rosen's warning loomed in the back of his mind, but making a living was crucial. The safari booking couldn't have come at a more opportune time. The London travel agent described the Milners as an elderly British couple. They were birding enthusiasts, which wasn't unusual. Botswana has a robust bird population. Birding safaris are common in southern Africa. When the booking agent recommended a retired ornithologist as their guide, they pitched a fit. They threatened cancelation unless the safari company guaranteed that Rigby Croxford would be their safari guide.

Rigby met his clients at the Maun Airport in neighboring Botswana. The minute he saw the Milners his paranoia dissipated. They were so typically English. The husband spoke in a toothy polished Eton accent. They were retired college professors. He wore knee-socks, desert boots and walked with a cane. His wife wore frumpish sandals and a matronly smock. Like most Brits, they were in dire need of dental work. They were saddled with the stereotypical British curse, bad teeth and ghastly skin. She had binoculars draped around her neck. He had wire-framed spectacles perched on the tip of his upturned nose. By any measure, they looked like an innocuous, charming couple. They told Rigby that he had been recommended by a friend of friend. Qualms about their hidden agenda were set aside.

For the first seven days, they skirted the outer edges of the Okavango Delta. They saw lilac-breasted rollers, rosette spoonbills, sun grebes, buntings and fifty different species. The Milners were delighted. At night, they drank wine as they chronicled the day's sightings in the pages of Roberts's Birds of Southern Africa.

The second half of the Milner's birding safari called for a dugout mokoro canoe excursion into the interior of the swamp. An island campsite had been leased. They hoped to see more elusive species like the buff-breasted sandpiper and the even rarer, Pel's fishing owl.

At the same time the Milner safari headed back to Maun to get resupplied, Dr. Christine Croxford finished up an emergency appendectomy. She peeled off the surgical gloves and struggled out of her operating gown. Looking out the window, she saw the long line of patients waiting to see her. And she still had her rounds to make. Her clinic was overflowing with aids patients. Africans referred to the terminal illness as the 'slow puncture'. The sufferers would slowly deflate much like a tire losing air. It would be another long day. Time for a tea break, she thought.

Between sips of tea she conferred with a surgical nurse. They heard a commotion outside.

Sergeant Moyo accompanied by four men had been prevented from entering the clinic by a nurse. Christine, who spoke fluent Shona, was incensed.

"What gives you the right to jump to the head of this queue?"

Moyo sneered. "This is an official visit, madam." He pushed passed her and barged in. Once inside, they encircled Christine. Moyo said, "We have an arrest warrant for your father."

Christine stood her ground. "You have no such thing. You're here to anger my father. Be careful what you wish for, Moyo. My father is not a man to be trifled with. You should know that by now."

Moyo shot her a wicked smile. He used his nightstick to outline her hip. Shocked, she stepped back, but the men standing behind her refused to budge. Moyo reached out and jostled her breast. The men groped her buttocks. Without warning, she struck Moyo with a cupped hand to his ear, which short-circuited his equilibrium. He went down in a heap. His men helped him up, but his legs wouldn't support him.

In retaliation, a man slapped Christine with enough force to knock her off her feet. Her scream brought the nurses. One nurse ran outside pleading for help. The enraged patients poured into the clinic. They swarmed over her tormentors like feeding lions. There seemed no cure for their fury. They dragged the policemen outside where the angry mob used their canes and walking sticks to beat them into submission. They kicked and stomped them with calloused feet. The women were much more violent than the men. It was a culmination of repressed anger.

Christine retrieved one of her father's hunting rifles. The shot she fired into the air stopped the beating. The crowd parted. Moyo had taken the worst of it. His face was reduced to a bloody pulp. His broken arm was bent at an impossible angle. He whimpered.

At Christine's instruction, the nurses carried the battered

policemen into the clinic on stretchers. She set Sergeant Moyo's broken and sutured his facial wounds. The others also required stitches. They begged for forgiveness.

Jed purchased supplies while the Milners shopped for native curios at an outdoor native market. Rigby sought refuge at the Wild Duck Inn, a favorite watering hole for safari guides, pilots and other serious boozers. Laughter filled the smoky air. Rigby sat at the bar chatting with two expatriated Rhodesians when he felt a firm hand on his shoulder. "Otto, what brings you to my wicked den of iniquity? Always figured you for a decent sort. When he saw the anxiety in Otto's face he said, "What's going on?"

Otto grabbed his arm and led him outside.

"Christine's beside herself. Thank God, I found you."

"Why?" Rigby asked.

Otto told him about the telephone call his daughter received from Lily Rosen. "Lily said and I quote, 'Beware of birders.'"

Rigby's jaw tightened. "That's it?"

Otto grimaced carefully around his false teeth. "That's all Lily said before hanging up."

He eyed Otto. "There's something you're not telling me."

Otto hesitated. "Sergeant Moyo paid Christine a visit. He...."

"C'mon Otto, give it to me straight. Is my daughter safe?"

Otto decided against giving him the details. To do so, might endanger his Rigby's life.

"She's fine. Her patients damn near killed Moyo and his men. Christine wound up treating Moyo."

Rigby scratched his chin stubble. It took him a moment to assimilate Lily's warning. "Otto, I want you to contact Christine. Tell her not to worry. Everything's under control on my end. Can you do that for me?"

"Of course. Say, do you..." Before Otto could finish, Rigby jumped into his Land Rover and drove away.

The Milners used their phony shopping spree to reassemble two weapons in the privacy of a gentlemen's loo. Suitcase handles doubled as barrels for two small caliber pistols. The trigger mechanisms were concealed in an inoperative Nikon telephoto lens. The cartridges were concealed in Mrs. Milner's custom jewelry.

Rigby found them at the native market. He watched the Milners approaching in the rearview mirror. Mrs. Milner was clutching her handbag. As she got closer, she stuck her hand into the bag. Rigby beeped the horn and waved at a group of tourists. He jumped out. "Jed, you drive. I'll ride in the back with Mrs. Milner," he said.

Mrs. Milner reached into her handbag. Rigby flinched and prepared to duck.

"How about taking a snap of us? She jerked out the camera and handed it to Rigby.

"With pleasure, madam," he said exhaling.

Jed and Rigby shared a hotel room that night. They took turns standing guard. Both agreed that if the Milners planned to waylay them, the canoe trip was the ideal place. By the time Rigby and Jed were listed as missing, their killers would be long gone.

Early the next morning, they set off in two canoes. Each canoe contained a Milner in the bows with Jed and Rigby paddling in the sterns. Supplies were stacked in the middle. Rigby insisted that the canoes keep a fifty-meter separation. This exceeded the effective range for most handguns.

Instead of paddling down a clearly defined waterway toward the campsite, Rigby led them in the opposite direction. Hippos had flattened narrow pathways in the tall papyrus grass. Water-bugs and brightly colored reed spiders stuck to the paddlers' clothing. Bullfrogs croaked. Juvenile tigerfish chased minnows into the shallows. Wading open-billed storks and snowy-white egrets took flight. They heard splashing from the swamp antelopes. The islands were marked by willowy phoenix palms. Huge crocodiles elevated themselves on bowed legs and waddled into the water. Smaller crocs exploded off the banks.

Two hours into the canoe trip, Milner yelled, "I say, Croxford, hope we're not lost? It all looks the same to me." He clutched his shoulder bag.

Rigby reassured him. "I'm well-acquainted with the Okavango, sir."

The problem was separating Mr. Milner from his shoulder bag, which Rigby believed contained a firearm. A mistake could be fatal. They paddled over a wide sandbar connected to an island. The water was deep and clear. Current eddies swirled lazily around the reeds. Rigby pushed with his paddle until the canoe's bow nuzzled up against the shoreline. Rigby motioned to disembark, but when Mr. Milner stood up Rigby shoved off with his paddle. Without his cane, Milner lost his footing and fell overboard. He came up sputtering for air. The current swept him just out of Rigby's reach, but Jed managed to grab the strap on Milner's shoulder bag. He jerked the bag free and tossed it to Rigby, who opened it and emptied the contents. A pistol hit the deck.

Rigby emitted a soft murmur. "What have we here? And I thought we were getting on so well."

Milner hung to the gunnels churning out incoherent profanities. The Eton accent had yielded to cockney. His wife never hesitated. She produced her weapon and commenced firing, but the canoe was a shaky platform. A bullet whizzed by Rigby's ear. She stood up, steadied herself and took better aim, but before she could fire Rigby vaulted over the side. Her next shot splintered wood. When he resurfaced he capsized her canoe. She came up disoriented. Jed snatched the pistol from her hand. Her language would have reddened a sailor's face.

The Milners beached the canoes at gunpoint. Everyone waded ashore. "Let me finish them," Jed pleaded. Rigby hesitated, and then he shook his head. Hard to explain their disappearance to the police, he thought.

Jed bailed out the flooded canoes while Rigby stood guard. "Dkari Sibanda hired you, didn't he?"

"Go fuck yourself," she hissed.

"Why not level with me. What's the point?"

"I said, to fuck off," she repeated more venomously.

"Such vulgarity from an English lady, I'm shocked beyond belief," Rigby heckled.

Mrs. Milner made an obscene hand gesture. "Stick this up your ass, Croxford."

Rigby and Jed paddled the canoes out into the channel leaving the Milners standing on the shoreline. Mrs. Milner yelled defiantly, "You shit-eating maggots haven't seen the last of us."

"Madam, if we do meet again, please rest assured my face will be the last thing you'll ever see in this lifetime, I promise you that. And the same goes for your husband, if he was in fact unlucky enough to have married you. You have my sincere sympathy, sir. I hope you both enjoy the rest of your birding experience." Rigby hurled the pistols at them. "Here, you'll need these. I wouldn't toddle off if I were you. Crocs aren't finicky about their diets."

By the time the Milners retrieved the weapons, Rigby and Jed had disappeared behind a wall of river reeds. Mrs. Milner's four-letter words carried on the water for what seemed like an eternity.

Possessing handguns is a serious crime in Botswana. The Botswana Defense Force arrested the Milners two days later. Mosquitoes and fear had ravaged the would-be assassins. They were delirious and bore no likeness to their passport photographs. The Milners were sentenced to two years in prison. Large bribes were paid. They served less than a week.

They vowed to never set-foot on African soil again.

The second incident occurred two weeks later in Zimbabwe. Rigby sat on his veranda in the predawn darkness enjoying his first cup of tea. Something didn't feel right. An unusual calm had set in. Even the crickets were silenced. He whistled for his Rhodesian ridgebacks, but they didn't come to him. Later that morning, he found his dogs hanging from a tree limb. Both animals had been disemboweled.

The senseless cruelty sealed an understanding between Rigby and his daughter. Christine accepted her father's opinion. They would never be safe as long as Dkari Sibanda was alive. Rigby was running out of cards to play. The best option was to lure Sibanda out into the open. The first step was to disappear into the wilderness.

Christine's last words to her father were, "Do whatever it takes, just end this thing once and for all."

JAMES GARDNER

JAMES GARDNER

24

The land between Botswana and Zimbabwe is painted in mottled shades of brown. The Kalahari Basin gets its name from the Tswana word *Kgala*, which means the great thirst. It's an unsympathetic world balanced between life and death where the weak are culled from the living. Energy is not squandered. Nothing moves midday except dust devils.

The San's ancestral land is a foreboding, inhospitable ecosystem, yet the Bushmen have survived there for over twenty thousand years. Geneticists agree that Bushmen are the original descendants of *Homo sapiens*. More recently, governments evicted Bushmen to supposedly protect the wildlife; the real reason was to provide security for the diamond concessions. The last legal permit to kill a Bushman on sight was issued in 1939. Most of them were exterminated by Dutch settlers, yet a few small bands manage to survive in the Kalahari. For Rigby, it was an ideal place to kill Dkari Sibanda.

The tarmac road contained too many potholes to avoid them. The kidney-jarring drive beat them into capitulation.

Rigby turned off onto a side road that quickly became a rutted animal trail. The fringes of the desert are pockmarked by kopjes or rocky outcroppings with boulders heaped in all sizes that have

[215]

JAMES GARDNER

been regurgitated from the earth's bowels. Rigby and Jed chose a kopje near an ancient salt pan as their campsite. It afforded a twenty-kilometer panoramic view. The pan was a perfect landing site for Otto Bern's resupply flights.

It was too late to make camp. They opted to sleep in the Land Rover. Days in the desert are stifling. Nights are bone-achingly cold. Their first night was sleepless.

The next day Jed discovered a granite cave in a kopje. The surrounding land was so sterile it took hours to gather enough wood for a fire. They spent the rest of the day preparing what would be their home for the foreseeable future. The first order of business was to rid the cave of poisonous snakes and scorpions.

That night they hunkered next to the campfire in their sleeping bags. The flickering flames illuminated prehistoric cave paintings depicting animals and traced human handprints.

"Brr. I forgot how bloody cold it gets in the desert," Rigby stammered.

Jed pointed at the prehistoric graffiti. "Who painted them?"

"Bushmen or the ancestors of Bushmen, I reckon. Before the Egyptians built the pyramids, no doubt."

"We call them the *Basarwa*—the people who have nothing," Jed said.

"Bloody fine trackers, that much I do know."

Jed couldn't disagree.

The morning was devoted to clearing a makeshift landing strip for Otto Bern's Piper.

As planned, Otto landed that afternoon without incident. He back-taxied his Cherokee, spun back around into the wind and shutdown the engine. Otto opened the door and lifted his prosthetic leg up onto the wing.

"Anything out of the ordinary happen?" Rigby yelled.

"Not really," Otto answered struggling to climb onto the wing. "Well, there was something rather odd, actually."

"What was that?" Rigby inquired.

Otto explained his initial suspicion that someone might have sabotaged his airplane. But after a thorough preflight, he dismissed the notion. "To tell you the truth, she never flew better. I could have sworn someone messed with my bird."

"I'm relieved. Anything happens to you, we're screwed. You're our only lifeline."

They unloaded the supplies, including two jerry cans of water. "What's our timeframe?" Otto asked.

"It depends," Rigby replied.

"On?" Otto asked.

"Two things, really. How long it takes Sibanda to find me. Or how long we can survive my cooking—weapons of mass destruction, actually."

Jed grinned.

Rigby reiterated his strategy to lure Dkari Sibanda into the open. Rumors had been circulated about Rigby's location. Sibanda was always wary, but hopefully his appetite for vengeance would be his undoing. Enticing him to use the helicopter would reduce his bodyguards from four to two.

Otto said, "My airport sources tell me Sibanda's pilot has been making inquiries as to your whereabouts. Make no mistake about it, he'll show up here sooner or later."

"We're ready for him," Rigby said, holding up his .458 Winchester. "See you in three days. Hey, don't forget the petro. We're running on air."

"Better let you two lovebirds get on with it," Otto said giving them thumbs up. He mouthed cheers and slammed the pilot's door.

For the first one hundred meters Otto's takeoff run was bouncy, but as he gained airspeed the Piper's wings provided lift which lessened the stress on the airframe. The Cherokee lifted off with distance to spare and banked for the return flight to Victoria Falls. They watched the airplane fade away into the afternoon haze.

Within seconds, the desert's solitude returned.

Jed and Rigby went about their separate duties. It was Rigby's turn to scavenge for firewood. He abandoned the Land Rover at the base of a sand dune. As he searched he came upon a herd of long-legged desert elephants. Dusting themselves in desert clay had colored them as white as cotton. All had ribs showing. The matriarch spun around and trumpeted. She shook her head like a dog shaking off water, but her challenge was half-hearted. The herd shuffled away in slow motion. After a short time they shimmered on the horizon like phantom schooners tacking on a mirrored sea. He witnessed a gemsbok standing alone under the shade of a camel-thorn tree. The black on grey antelope lowered its horns and snorted, but it didn't move. Surrendering shade in the desert is a death sentence.

On the drive back he found the charred remains of a bonfire. Jed needs to see this, he said to himself. As he approached the kopje he grew curious about the absence of smoke. What happened to our campfire, he wondered.

With the sticks and limbs strapped to his back, Rigby started the backbreaking climb to the cave. He stopped halfway up to catch his breath. The setting sun was as orange as an egg yolk. He scanned the horizon. The coast was clear. Suddenly, seeds of apprehension resurfaced. Rigby dumped his load and scrambled up through the rocks.

As he stooped to enter the cave he noticed the overturned jerry cans. Jed was lying on his side. Rigby rolled him over. His cheeks were cold to the touch. Jed's blood-red eyes were open. Pink foam bubbled from his nose. He placed his fingers against Jed's neck and felt no pulse. Rigby's worst fears washed over him. His friend of forty years was dead.

Has to be a snake, he thought. The Kalahari is home to the most poisonous reptiles in the world. He examined Jed's arms and legs. He stared at the empty jerry cans. Jed's dying act was to kick over the water containers. He squatted for a closer look. Jed's tongue was blue, a symptom of cyanide poisoning. He remembered Otto's premonition about his airplane being vandalized. Someone had poisoned the jerry cans of water. That someone had to be Dkari Sibanda. He knuckled the fatigue from his temples. This is my doing, he thought.

Ingesting cyanide causes the victim to endure an agonizing death. He imagined Jed in his final death-throes. Racked by what had to be horrific pain, Jed made sure Rigby would not suffer his same fate by knocking over the water containers. Rigby picked up one the empty cans and hurled against the wall.

Rigby found sleep elusive. A mental picture of Dkari Sibanda kept reappearing. Jed's death had besieged him. He could think of nothing but killing.

Otto was due back in three days. Rigby drained the life-sustaining fluid from his Land Rover's cooling system that morning. Rationing just might keep me alive, he thought, allowing himself a sip of the rusty water.

Rigby abandoned the cave after two nights. The cave paintings were completely obscured by blowflies. Jed's corpse was rotting. Hopes for a proper funeral for his friend had ended. He buried Jed the next day in a shallow grave underneath a desert acacia. Spotted hyenas are grave desecrators. He piled stones on the gravesite as a deterrent.

He consumed the last drops of radiator water on the morning of the third day. That afternoon he walked to the landing site to wait for Otto. He stared at the harsh blue sky hoping to see that familiar dot. A few times he thought he saw it, but his optimism was dashed. The dot proved to be a vulture.

25

Otto's flight plan listed Kasane as his final destination, but he overflew the airport and set a course for the Botswana border. The land flattened as he approached the Kalahari region.

His Cherokee-six was overloaded, but he'd managed the takeoff as he'd done a million times. He looked forward to spending the night in the desert and getting drunk with Croxford, which was something he'd also done a million times. Well, maybe not a million, he thought, correcting himself. He glanced at the two bottles of Dewar's scotch strapped down in the copilot's seat and smiled at the thought of Rigby's favorable reaction.

The barren bush veldt passing beneath him looked desolate. He checked the flight instruments. The fuel gauges were bouncing on empty, but they hadn't worked properly in months. I need to get these sorted one of these days, he thought. He'd topped off the fuel tanks that night, but hadn't dipped them before takeoff. He remembered telling his flying students, "Complacency is a pilot's enemy, especially when it comes to checking your fuel." He recalculated the fuel burn again. He reassured himself; I've got enough fuel onboard to make this trip three times. He chastised himself vowing never to make the mistake again. Always check the damn fuel before taking off, he thought.

The last waypoint before Rigby's campsite was a large rock

kopje with an ancient baobab tree growing at its base. He noted the time as the landmark passed underneath him. He changed headings. The desert floor was scored by crisscrossing animal migrations. Only twenty minutes to touchdown, he thought looking down. The engine sputtered. Otto turned on the boost pump and switched to the outboard fuel tanks.

The sound of the engine changed ever so slightly. The change would have gone unnoticed by most pilots, but not Otto. He was an experienced airplane mechanic as well as a skilled bush pilot. His fellow flying enthusiasts said Otto had aviation oil circulating in his veins. He checked the tachometer. The engine had dropped fifty revolutions. He pushed the throttle back to the cruise setting. Bloody throttle cable has loosened, he hoped.

The engine misfired. He activated the boost pump again and scanned the engine instruments. Oil pressure was normal. Cylinder temperature was in the green. Everything seemed in good working order. The engine raced and then it sputtered. Finally, it stopped with a clunk. Like that, is it! Otto yelled. He initiated the restart process, but deep down he knew it was a waste of time. He turned the key. The engine turned over but wouldn't fire. Just as I thought, dead as Kelsey's nuts. The way it quit said fuel starvation.

The outboard tanks are empty. Someone drained my fuel supply, he realized.

Otto had survived three dead-stick-landings during his flying career, one of which had cost him an ear. He spoke aloud rehearsing the emergency landing procedure. At three thousand feet I've got six minutes of gliding time. I can cover six to eight miles if all goes by the book. He checked his position on the GPS. It was twenty nautical miles to the campsite.

After tuning the radio to the emergency frequency, he set the glide rate at eighty knots.

He assessed his survival chances. At least fire won't be a problem—bloody fuel tanks are empty. He remembered the cans of petrol in the cargo bay. Like all pilots, Otto was terrified of being trapped in a burning fuselage. He grabbed the Scotch bottles and tossed them into the backseat. Otto undid his artificial leg and strapped it under the copilot's seatbelt. I'll need my leg intact more than the booze. He smiled thinking about Rigby's castigation about saving his leg versus the whiskey. Time slowed down to a snail's pace. In Otto's mind's eye he saw his departed relatives, but he shook his head to clear the image. Better concentrate on the landing, he cautioned himself.

Two minutes to touchdown. What appeared smooth from three thousand feet now looked uneven from one thousand. The land was strewn with animal burrows and knolls. What he feared most was hitting a termite mound. Landing into the wind was preferable, but not always possible. The absence of a headwind meant landing at a higher speed. Otto hit the starter until the two-bladed propeller turned horizontal to protect it from getting damaged.

One minute to go. Otto banked sharply to avoid a mound. He crossed himself, cinched down his seatbelt, pulled in full flaps and pitched up the nose until the airspeed hovered at sixty. The right wheel contacting a rise caused the right wing to lift skyward. He leveled the wings and braced himself. The Cherokee bounced three times before plowing into a sand dune. There was a painful screech from metal tearing. It nosed over, hovered momentarily and then fell backwards landing on its wheels. A massive sand cloud engulfed the crash. In spite of his best efforts to brace himself, Otto's head snapped forward striking the yoke. And then everything went black.

JAMES GARDNER

26

The setting sun cast long shadows before disappearing in a flaming orange display. The desert temperature dropped with the sun. Nightjars chasing insects made whooshing sounds. A shooting star streaked across the darkening sky. It was now too dark for Otto Bern to land his airplane. Rigby hoped Otto had incurred a mechanical breakdown, but deep down he feared the worst. By the end of the fourth day, Rigby suspected that Otto was another victim of Dkari Sibanda's treachery. He drained the last drops of water from the vehicle's cooling system. The Land Rover was running on fumes, which made driving out of the desert impossible. His only option was to sit tight and hope to be rescued. He used the remaining petrol to fuel a signaling fire.

One time he thought he saw an aircraft, but it was a cruel creation of his imagination. He slept in the Land Rover at night and used it to block the sun during the day. When he looked in a side mirror he hardly recognized himself. His lips were cracked. His face was gaunt and blistered. His eyes were vacant. The need for revenge was the only thing keeping him alive.

On the fifth day he shot a desert hare and drank its blood. The following day he was too weak to walk. He lapsed in and out of consciousness. He dreamed about Bushmen.

Honey-colored, bare-breasted women with babies strapped on their backs digging for tubers and wild onions, their foreheads fringed in colorful beads. The children gathered termites and ate them. Tattooed men with their hair twisted in peppercorn sprigs stood over him in a circle. He looked up at them. Their weathered faces seamed by deep wrinkles looked solemn. They chanted their tribal mantra in a modulating harmony. 'On the day we die a soft breeze will wipe our footprints from the sand. When the wind dies down who will tell the timelessness that once we walked this way in the dawn of time.' The dream ended with a vision of Helen beckoning him with open arms.

Kgosi and his brother, Xamseb, were tracking a gemsbok when they saw a wispy curl of smoke on the horizon. Kgosi squatted to examine the condition of the gemsbok's droppings. He crushed the dung pellets between his fingers checking the moisture content. The hunters knew their quarry was near, but the smoke concerned them. Bushmen are persecuted for hunting in the Kalahari. They decided to suspend their hunt and investigate the source of the smoke.

The Bushmen approached the Land Rover with care. When they saw Rigby laying face up in the dirt they became even more guarded. They kept their distance and tossed pebbles at him. He was so unresponsive they assumed he was dead.

Kgosi bent over Rigby, and then he abruptly stood up.

Xamseb placed his ear next to Rigby's nose. The brothers conversed in a sing-song exchange punctuated by harmonic clicks and clucks.

Kgosi retrieved a dirty bed sheet from the Land Rover. After urinating on the sheet they draped it over Rigby's body. They fanned the sheet. The resulting condensation lowered Rigby's body temperature. He stirred and mumbled.

For Bushmen, water is the very essence of life. Wasting water on a dying man was seen as foolhardy. They argued about this wastefulness, but Kgosi prevailed. He uncorked one of the ostrich egg canteens he carried on a leather belt. He inserted a grass-straw into the opening and placed it to Rigby's lips. Rigby sucked on the straw like a calf nursing on a cow's teat. He opened his eyes, but he was too weak to speak. He still wasn't sure he was alive.

Kgosi stood with his clubfoot braced against the knobby knee of his other leg like a resting wood stork. Their sandals were made from truck tires. They carried bows and quivers of poisoned arrows. His brother dropped to his heels like a grasshopper. He placed his hand on Rigby's forehead. Rigby grabbed his hand and held it to his cheek as a sign of gratitude.

Rigby spoke hoarsely in what he thought was their native tongue. "Please help me."

Kgosi grinned. "Your Khoisan is very bad. We speak some English and the language of the Boors."

Rigby shaded his eyes. He spoke in Afrikaans. "I know you. You are Kgosi, the rhino killer."

Kgosi's expression showed he was offended. He shook his head vehemently. "I am Kgosi, the leader of my clan. He is Xamseb, the lion. "We hunt to eat. I would never kill a rhino. To do so, would offend the God, Kaang." Kgosi's brother nodded.

"We found your spoor around a dying rhino," Rigby charged pointing at Kgosi's deformed foot.

"Now, I remember you—the man who shoots at flying machines. What happened to your friend?"

Rigby pointed at Jed's grave. "Poisoned. The killer's name is Dkari Sibanda."

A light of recognition flashed in Kgosi's eyes. His brother looked away.

"You know him, don't you?" Rigby's question alarmed Kgosi and his brother. They switched to their native language to discuss the matter. Kgosi removed his woolen ski cap. The brothers bowed their heads in reverence. "Yes, we know the man who killed your friend."

Kgosi explained that they stumbled on the blood trail left by the dying rhino. And that he tracked the rhino killer and watched him hide the rhino's horn in a dead baobab tree. He decided to exploit his good fortune by selling the rhino horn to Dkari Sibanda. Later, he was disappointed to learn that the money Sibanda paid him was worthless.

"So, the poachers killed that rhino."

"No, baas, it was Moyo, the policeman."

"He's the one who arrested me." Rigby said more for himself.

"I saw what he did."

Rigby tried to stand up, but he couldn't. He slid down the side of the Rover. So that's why the rangers didn't show up, he thought. Moyo threatened them. No wonder he was so pissed off. Losing the rhino horn cost him plenty.

Kgosi's brother took seeds and crushed hoodia cactus from the dappled tortoise shell he carried on a belt around his waist. He wrapped the herbs in a dried leaf. He instructed Rigby to place the leaf underneath his tongue, which he did. Within minutes, Rigby had regained enough strength to stand up. His mouth tingled.

The hunger pangs were gone. Even his thirst was quenched.

Rigby retrieved a map from the Land Rover and spread it across the Land Rover's bonnet. The Bushmen looked over his shoulder listening politely as he described Otto Bern's airplane and the resupply flight that never materialized. "I'm afraid my pilot friend has been killed."

Kgosi stroked his sparse chin whiskers. "Does your friend walk on one or two legs?"

"Otto has one leg," Rigby stated regaining his strength.

"Your friend isn't dead. He's out there." He pointed in a direction that would have approximated Otto's inbound heading.

"How do you know this?" Rigby asked.

The brothers giggled. "We saw your friend yesterday. We traded him ganja weed for whiskey."

"Why isn't he with you?" Rigby asked.

"He refuses to leave his flying machine," Kgosi said. He gave Rigby more water.

"He has great trouble walking." To make his point, Xamseb hopped around on one leg. The imitation made his brother giggle.

"How far is this place?" Rigby asked looking out into the desert.

After conferring, Kgosi's brother said, "Not so far."

Rigby was well aware of the Bushmen's hazy concept of time and space. "How long will it take me to walk there?"

They sized Rigby up and down. "If we leave now we could be there before the sun disappears. It would take you much longer,"

Kgosi said. Xamseb concurred with his brother's assessment by nodding.

"Will you take me there?"

"*Ja*," the brothers replied in unison.

Kgosi took the point. Rigby followed him into the desert as sightless as a blind man. Xamseb brought up the rear carrying Rigby's Winchester. Kgosi carried the bows, quivers and the water. The brothers smiled when Rigby referred to his land map. Their desert maps were indelibly printed in their memory banks. Like ground squirrels hiding nuts, Bushmen bury ostrich egg canteens as emergency water reserves. How they locate the caches without using landmarks has always been a mystery.

Rigby consumed more water than both Bushmen combined. The brothers allowed this excess to continue until they believed he was sufficiently hydrated. Rigby accepted their rationing. Each time they stopped to dig up ostrich egg canteens, they fed Rigby more herbs.

From time to time, Xamseb stooped to dig up tubers. They chewed the roots as they walked. Rigby felt re-energized, but it didn't last. After three hours of hard walking, his legs went numb. When Kgosi saw Rigby stumble, he said, "We will rest here until the moon is high. You will see your friend before the sun rises."

Rigby was too exhausted to sleep. He collapsed next to the campfire with his back leaning against a termite mound. Rigby was about to speak when Kgosi said, "I think the man who killed your friend is the same man who killed your wife."

Rigby gritted his emotional teeth. "How do you know this?"

Kgosi said, "You spoke to your wife in your dreams when we found you." He looked very sad. He was thinking about the loss of his own wife. "This man you want to kill is dangerous. He is as greedy as a honey-badger feeding at a beehive. Be careful or he will kill you too."

"I don't care what happens to me. I aim to finish him." Xamseb rolled a homemade cigarette. He encouraged Rigby to take a puff, which he did. Rising blue smoke made his eyes water. Almost immediately, he fell into a deep sleep.

Kgosi and Xamseb allowed Rigby to sleep for two hours. As they watched him sleep they argued about what they should do with him. Xamseb wanted to leave him at the Land Rover, but Kgosi wouldn't have it. Soon, they would be responsible for two white men, both of whom had no knowledge of surviving in the desert. One couldn't even walk. Taking on such burdens could be life-threatening. We can barely could feed ourselves, Xamseb pointed out. How can we feed them? Kgosi dismissed his brother's fears. Surely, their God, Manta, would give them guidance in this matter.

Kgosi gently tapped Rigby's shoulder pointing up at the crescent moon. Rigby stood up and yawned.

They marched single file into the night. The air was cold and dry. The only sounds were the hair-raising cackles from hyenas and the yelps of a hunting jackal. After walking for two hours they saw the distant glow from a campfire. As they got closer, the flames illuminated Otto's crashed airplane.

Otto Bern hobbled out of the darkness. "Bloody hell, what took you so long, Croxford? I see my bush-friends found you." Rigby and Otto hugged each other. He handed Rigby the bottle of Scotch. I've been saving this for you."

"Cheers." Rigby took a long swig and gave the bottle to Kgosi. "Never thought I'd see your ugly mug again, Otto."

"So, where's Jed?" Otto asked looking into the night.

JAMES GARDNER

Instead of replying, Rigby looked down. There wasn't a need to answer. His expression said everything.

Otto shook his head. "I was afraid of this. Sibanda's dirty work, no doubt. He had someone sabotage my bird. How did he get to Jed?"

"The water you delivered contained cyanide."

"Sweet Jesus, I'm sorry. Sibanda's funeral will be the happiest day of my life."

"He doesn't deserve a funeral. I aim to squash him like a vile tick."

"It couldn't happen to a more deserving son-of-a-bitch. I have one fear."

Rigby felt the weariness seeping back into his body. "Which is?"

"I might not live long enough to witness his death. God knows, Jed was a good one. I know you'll miss him—we all will."

Rigby sat down with his back against the Piper's fuselage. "Indeed. Telling his wives won't be easy."

Otto said, "Can't say I envy you. Bloody awful stuff."

"How're we gonna get out of here, Otto?"

Otto removed his false teeth and cleaned them with an acacia thorn. "That one's easy enough. Fly out, of course."

Rigby never answered. He fell into dreamless sleep. Within seconds he was snoring. Otto took off his coat and draped it over his friend's shoulders.

[232]

The next day Otto explained that whoever vandalized his aircraft had disconnected the fuel selector valve to the outboard tanks. He hadn't run out of avgas. He had unwittingly switched to unconnected fuel tanks. He had already repaired the fuel-line linkage. The crash-landing had bent the left main-gear strut. The wheel pants had been torn off, but they weren't necessary for flight. Now that he had the manpower to lift the left wing, it was an easy fix. Luckily, he had landed in a relatively flat spot in the desert. If Kgosi and his brother could flatten a few termite mounds, he felt he had sufficient room for a takeoff.

They had been working for two full hours before the pale promise of dawn cracked the horizon. Kgosi and Xamseb worked feverishly to flatten four termite mounds. Otto used the barrel of Rigby's Winchester as a lever to straighten the landing gear strut.

They were jockeying Otto's Piper into a takeoff position, when Kgosi shouted, "*Beweeg voel.*" He said, 'hovering bird' in Afrikaans, but Otto knew he meant helicopter.

"I was afraid of this. Quick, get into the backseat, Croxford." Otto covered Rigby with a cargo tarp. "You two get out of here," Otto said shooing Kgosi and his brother. Otto draped himself over a wing. He whispered out of the corner of his mouth to Croxford, "Better pray it's the search and rescue copter. If it's Sibanda, we're shit out of luck."

Dkari Sibanda ordered his pilot to hover over the crash site. Otto was buffeted by the helicopter's rotor-wash, but he didn't move a muscle. Sibanda grabbed the barrel of his bodyguard's Kalashnikov, "No need wasting ammo—he's dead. Leave him be."

The bodyguard pointed at the Bushmen running away. "What about them?"

"Shoot those dung beetles!" Sibanda screamed patting the man's arm.

The helicopter dipped its nose, banked ninety degrees and took up the chase. When Kgosi and Xamseb heard the approaching helicopter, they ran off in opposite directions. Xamseb stumbled and fell. He jumped to his feet and was running flat out, but the mishap made him a better target of opportunity. The pilot was after him in a flash. He turned the helicopter broadside. The bodyguard slid his door open. The first round of bullets kicked up dirt behind Xamseb. He zigzagged like a gazelle eluding a cheetah. The Bushman lost his footing again and went down in a cloud of dust. Sibanda found this hilarious. He howled with laughter. The pilot raced ahead and spun back around, but Xamseb changed directions again. Sibanda grabbed his bodyguard's weapon and opened his door. Helicopter sliding sideways gave him an easy shot. The burst riddled Xamseb's back severing his spine. He fell paralyzed, but he was still alive. He pulled himself along with his arms for a few feet and then he gave up and rolled over. Sibanda emptied the clip into Xamseb's body until he stopped moving.

The pilot turned his attention on Kgosi. He gained altitude and began searching the area. The helicopter circled for a short time, but Sibanda quickly lost interest. The helicopter disappeared over the horizon.

When Kgosi heard the gunshots, he dove into an abandoned aardvark den burrowed into the base of a termite mound. He climbed out and ran to his brother.

Rigby and Otto found Kgosi rocking his dead brother in his arms. Tears streaked his wrinkled dusty face. Otto shook his head saying, "Xamseb was all the family he had left. His entire clan has been exterminated. It's tragic. Bushmen are such gentle souls. The munts treat them like vermin. Hard to figure."

Rigby said, "Otto, if we manage to get out of here alive, you need to stay clear of me. People around me are dying at an alarming rate. I'm running out of friends."

"Nonsense, Croxford. Like I said before, I intend to toast Sibanda's death."

Rigby thought for a minute. "Killing that bastard will probably be my undoing. Can't see myself surviving that one, not with his bodyguards."

Otto said, "Perhaps—perhaps not. Tell him what you told me." He looked at Kgosi.

Kgosi blinked back his hatred. "Trust me, *Baba*. I know how to kill this devil."

After they buried Kgosi's brother, Otto prepared his airplane for the flight out of the desert. All nonessentials were offloaded. The jerry cans of petrol would make the trip. Otto planned on stopping at Rigby's camp. Recovering the Land Rover was crucial to Kgosi's plan. The passenger seats would be left behind. A lighter airplane had a better chance of making a short-field takeoff. It didn't take much coaxing to get Kgosi to agree to come along. The death of his brother had stiffened his determination. Killing Dkari trumped his fear of airplanes.

Otto warmed up the engine. "Hold on tight, mates." He brought the engine up to full power and stood on the brakes. The Cherokee chomped on the bit like a racehorse at the gate. When he released the brakes, the Piper moved slowly at first and then it steadily gained speed. Otto jerked back on the yoke to prevent damage to the nose-wheel. The Piper bumped and bounced over the uneven ground like a bronco bucking on its hind legs. Without seats Rigby and Kgosi were tossed about in the back like rag dolls. At forty knots the takeoff run got smoother, but they were running out of level ground. He veered slightly to avoid a large termite mound. The left wheel hit a grassy knoll and launched the Cherokee, but without sufficient airspeed the airplane refused to fly and touched down again. Otto added two more notches of flaps. Grudgingly, the aging Cherokee lifted off. Otto yelled triumphantly, "Looks like we cheated death again, Croxford!"

They covered the ten miles to Rigby's campsite in less than five minutes. He flew around the kopje. Something he saw was upsetting enough to warrant a closer look. He circled again before he landed. Otto had seen a helicopter's skid-marks.

After Otto landed, he turned to Rigby and asked, "Didn't you tell me you piled rocks on Jed's grave?"

"That's right. Why do you ask?"

"You should have used heavier stones. The hyenas have been busy." Rigby protested. "Impossible. The stones *were* heavy."

The scene was horrifying. Human footprints around the gravesite indicated that someone had exhumed Jed's corpse. The defilers hadn't bothered to rebury his remains. During the night, hyenas had fed on the cadaver. Even his femurs and hip sockets had been crushed and consumed. Only the crown of Jed's skull and his booted feet were still intact. A large blood stain marked the hyenas' feeding frenzy.

Otto and Kgosi watched Rigby dig a burial pit and spread dirt over what was left of Jed. When he finished his grim work, he stood over the grave for a long time.

Otto joined Rigby at the gravesite. "May I say something?"

"Please do."

"You're determined to get yourself killed, aren't you?"

"I have to do *something*," Rigby said. They walked together to the Land Rover.

"You might as well hand me your rifle. Sibanda will have you killed before you fire the first shot."

"At this point, I don't give a shit." Rigby chambered a round into his Winchester. He climbed into the Land Rover and started the engine.

Otto stood in front of the Land Rover. "It's a bloody shame, that's all I'm saying."

"Get out of my way, Otto."

"And let you piss your life away, no way. What about your daughter, Christine, and her son? More importantly, who am I suppose to get drunk with. Especially, now that Penny has gone to the other side. Damn selfish of you, Croxford. That's all I'm saying."

A humorless grin pinched the corners of Rigby's mouth. He turned off the engine and placed his hands on the steering wheel. Without looking at Otto, he said, "All right, you win. Let's hear it."

"It's not my plan, old boy. It's Kgosi's plan. But I have to say, it's so damn clever, it made my heart sing."

James Gardner

27

Otto Bern flew his airplane to the Maun Airport in Botswana, where he waited for Rigby's call. If Kgosi's plan backfired, he was prepared to reenter Zimbabwe and fly everyone out of the country. Rigby and Otto faced the reality of living out their lives in exile. Returning to Zimbabwe under a Sibanda-led government would mean death sentences.

Rigby and Kgosi drove out into the desert. The Bushman gave him directions, which he followed without argument. In time, the terrain turned uphill into a rolling savanna. What had been sandy was now peppered by camel-thorn acacia and horned melon trees.

After driving for another two hours, he asked Rigby to stop. He got out of the Land Rover and began searching a sandy area with a few lonely acacias. The leafless trees had been stripped by foraging elephants. Rigby walked behind Kgosi, giving him space. The Bushman mumbled to himself and appeared to be in a hypnotic trance. He stopped dead in his tracks and pointed at twirling marks in the sand. "What I seek is hiding under that tree."

Rigby scratched his beard. "Which tree? They all look the same?"

Kgosi broke off a tree limb with a fork at one end. Using the stick as a probe, he began prying the rotting bark off the base of the acacia. Something made him jump back. Rigby had no trouble retreating. No snake in the Kalahari can evoke fear like a black mamba. An angry mamba can move faster than most people can run. Kgosi had disturbed a nest of two mating mambas. The female was over four meters long. The male was a bit shorter. The female struck first. She shot out of the den, rose up and opened her jaws displaying an inky black mouth as a warning. The male mamba slithered away, but Kgosi was after him like a mongoose. He pinned the snake's coffin-shaped head with his forked stick and shoveled it into a burlap bag. The hissing female lunged at him, but he used his stick to fend off the lightning quick strike. Her vertical catlike eyes fixated on him. She struck again, but this time Kgosi pinned her head to the ground. The enraged mamba twisted and rolled up the stick. Kgosi dropped her into a separate bag and tied the opening shut. He tried to hand the burlap bags to Rigby, who recoiled. The prank was not well-received, which made Kgosi grin.

Rigby and Kgosi drove all night to enter the Chizarira Game Reserve under the cover of darkness. They slipped past the ranger station unseen. At daybreak they drove to the spot where Michael Sibanda had been accidently killed in the shootout. The banks of the contaminated waterhole were littered with bleaching elephant bones. The carrion eaters had abandoned the waterhole. A few magpies picked over the remains.

From the waterhole, Kgosi led Rigby to the ancient baobab tree where he sold the rhino horn to Dkari Sibanda. They went about their separate jobs in silence. Rigby used a machete to cut hook-thorn branches. At Kgosi's instruction, he interlaced the thorny limbs around the baobab tree leaving only a narrow passageway leading to the tree and a hidden escape route.

After building a fire, Kgosi dug at the bases of several blackthorn acacia trees. Digging for two hours he amassed a collection of insect larvae. When he admonished Rigby for standing too close, he didn't argue. San hunters tip their arrows with the deadly poison extracted from the larvae of colorful leaf beetles. The poison is so toxic they spread the paste on the arrow shafts and not the heads to prevent accidents.

The next step was delicate. Kgosi squeezed each larva expelling a gooey green liquid into an ostrich shell that he held over the fire. He chewed acacia bark and spat into the pot. The thickening mixture turned black.

Now came the most dangerous part of his plan. He crawled on his hands and knees into the narrow opening to the baobab tree and began painstakingly painting the needle-sharp thorns with the sticky poisonous substance. It took him a long time to complete his work. A few times he stood up and stretched his back. As Rigby watched, he marveled at Kgosi's ingenuity. How many have died perfecting this poison, he wondered. No wonder Bushmen were the first rung on the human evolutionary ladder.

The last task was the easiest. Kgosi walked around and reentered the escape route from the other end. He placed the two burlap bags containing the black mambas into a tree hollow. On the way out he swept away his footprints with some twigs tied together.

The trap was baited.

It was just before daybreak when Rigby parked the Land Rover a few kilometers from the ranger compound. Rigby said, "Good luck, my brother. Remember what we talked about. And don't let the game warden bully you." They shook hands. Kgosi climbed out and disappeared into the trees.

When the game warden walked from the outhouse after his morning constitutional, he was surprised to find Kgosi sitting under a tree. He said, "So it's the great Kgosi, the king of the yellow monkey clan. You're a long way from home. To what do I owe this honor?"

His mockery made Kgosi angry, but he held his temper in check. "I wish to talk to Minister Sibanda." He held his hand to his ear indicating he meant by telephone.

"Anything you have to say to him, you can say to me."

Kgosi repeated the words Rigby had given him verbatim. "The minister warned me you might say these words. What I have to say is for the big boss to hear, not you."

The warden was furious. He muttered a volley of Shona curse words under his breath. "Stay here." The rangers came outside and began jeering Kgosi. The Bushman ignored them.

After a short time, the game warden returned. He handed Kgosi a mobile telephone. The Bushman had to be shown how to speak into the phone. He turned his back and spoke almost inaudibly, which added to the warden's foul disposition. He finished his conversation and handed the mobile back to the warden, who snarled, "Someday, I'll catch you poaching in my reserve, Mister High and Mighty. Let's see how much you like living in Hwange Prison."

The game warden reentered the building and slammed the door in Kgosi's face.

Rigby and the Bushman spent the next three hours driving on the bone-shaking rutted road to reach the waterhole. After hiding the Land Rover, Rigby climbed the same hill overlooking the spot where Sibanda's son had been killed. Kgosi waited in the shade under a teak tree.

The hours passed slowly. Shading his eyes, Rigby looked up at the sun. He was about to give up when he heard the distant rhythmic thumping of a helicopter. Kgosi walked out from underneath the tree and waved to him.

The Bell Jet-Ranger hovered briefly, pitched nose up and landed near the waterhole. Both passenger doors flew open. Dkari Sibanda and Uncle Mao disembarked. They were followed by a short blocky man carrying an AK-47. Instinctively, Kgosi ducked under the spinning rotor-blades and walked forward to meet them.

As Rigby watched he realized the meeting was becoming heated. Sibanda threw up his arms in disgust. The Chinaman strode back to helicopter. The man armed with the rifle, jammed the barrel against Kgosi's throat. Without warning, Sibanda sucker-punched Kgosi, knocking the little Bushman to the ground. He stood over him yelling. Kgosi scrambled to his feet. The quarreling became even more animated.

Rigby aimed his Winchester. He put the crosshairs on a spot between Sibanda's eyes. He was about to pull the trigger when the Chinaman reentered his field of vision. Mao stood between Sibanda and Kgosi. He seemed to be negotiating a settlement. The meeting wasn't as lively.

Bookending Kgosi, the three men walked back to the idling helicopter. This wasn't part of the plan. The plan was for Kgosi to lead them to the baobab tree on foot. This changed everything. The first rule of combat is never discard the ability to improvise. Rigby scrambled down the back of the hill and ran to his hidden Land Rover. He chased after the helicopter, but within seconds it flew out of sight.

Kgosi took them on a roundabout flight to the ambush site. He knew Rigby would drive the Land Rover to the baobab tree. By stalling, he hoped to give Rigby more time. Sibanda grew impatient. He grabbed his bodyguard's weapon and pointed it at Kgosi. "Either you find that tree or we will see if you can fly." The Chinaman swung the passenger door open. Air and noise rushed in. The Bushman glanced down. The bodyguard pushed him toward the open door. Kgosi's face showed abject panic. Sibanda and Mao found this comical.

Inspired by Sibanda's threat, Kgosi directed the pilot to land in a clearing five hundred meters away from the baobab tree. He used a winding ramble to reach the tree. Sibanda, who was sweating copiously, had to stop a few times to catch his breath. The Chinaman jokingly admonished him for lack of stamina.

When Kgosi spoke to Sibanda on the mobile telephone, he said he had two large rhino horns for sale. But this time, he would only accept American money. The demand helped validate his claim. At a minimum, the horns would fetch three quarters of a million dollars. It was too much of an enticement to ignore. Sibanda had no intention of paying Kgosi. As soon as he had the horns in his possession, he had instructed his bodyguard to shoot the Bushman, which is what Rigby predicted he would do. Sibanda had included Uncle Mao as a partner to facilitate a quick sale.

"What we seek is hidden in the same tree as the last time," Kgosi indicated. Sibanda said to him, "You go first." He motioned to his bodyguard to follow the Bushman.

The bodyguard clicked his weapon on full automatic. The helicopter pilot and Uncle Mao brought up the rear.

Kgosi navigated the narrow passageway carefully avoiding the poisoned hook-thorns.

Sibanda, Mao and the pilot were so overcome by curiosity and greed; they charged into the thicket like rutting bull elephants. "Get out of my way," Sibanda bellowed pushing Kgosi aside. The razor-sharp hook thorns slashed legs and arms. They cursed the thorns and plowed straight ahead into the thicket.

The ancient baobab's trunk had been ravished by feeding elephants. As Sibanda looked into the rotting hollow, Kgosi slipped around behind the tree. He found the escape route and ran. He expected to hear shots fired, but his victims were so mesmerized they never saw him slip away.

Kgosi had added heavy stones to the burlap bags to enhance their weight. Sibanda handed one of the bags to Mao. He hefted his bag up and down observing, "These horns are bigger than the last one. We'll make a fortune." He licked his bulbous pink lips as he spilled his bag's contents in the dirt. At the same time, Mao also dumped his contents on the ground. Jostling the black mambas in the burlap bags enraged the snakes. They came out striking at anything that moved. Sibanda was so overcome by fear, he froze. He screamed and tried to run, but his legs wouldn't obey him. The female mamba's strike was faster than a speeding bullet. She went straight for Sibanda's enormous belly. She struck him again and again, her inch long fangs pumping massive doses of the neurotoxic venom into his body. He fell immobilized unable to fend off the vicious bites to his face and neck. His convulsions snapped his incisors off at the stumps. Sibanda cried out for his mother in Shona, "*Amai vangu.*" He had seen the face of death.

The bodyguard fared no better. He fired his rifle, but at close quarters he missed the snakes. He was bitten on both calves. The smaller mamba latched onto his ankle like an English bulldog defending a bone. He grabbed the mamba and tried to fling it, but the snake twisted around and buried its fangs into his forearm.

He also collapsed paralyzed from the neck down.

Their venom depleted, the black mambas slithered away unharmed.

Mao and the pilot had avoided the snakebites, but their pants were shredded by Kgosi's poison-tipped hook-thorns. The poison raced through their bloodstreams. Mao picked up the bodyguard's weapon and ran after the pilot. He spewed obscenities in Mandarin.

The pilot yelled, "We can't just leave them."

"You fly me now or I shoot you," Mao threatened idiotically. He saw Kgosi crouching in the trees. "Wait! I wanna kill that nigger." He engaged a cartridge into the rifle and pushed the door open.

The pilot started the engine. As he waited for the turbine to spool up, he glanced over at Mao. The Chinaman's lips had turned blue. It was the first sign of cyanosis. His red blood cells were being robbed of life sustaining oxygen. He was slowly suffocating. He was too weak to aim the rifle. After firing wildly, he dropped the weapon.

"A snake bit you," the pilot slobbered, misdiagnosing Mao's condition.

Mao inadvertently switched to Mandarin again. "You fly me hospital now." His horrified face had taken on a bluish hue. His hands trembled. He tried to say something, but couldn't speak. His head slumped forward.

The helicopter lifted off and started to climb out, but the pilot's motor reflexes were impaired by the poison. His irregular breathing was labored. He had trouble moving his right arm. He grabbed the collective lever in an attempt to regain control, but his uncoordinated effort was clumsy. The vibrating helicopter tipped ninety degrees sideways. The rotor blades smacking the ground splintered into pieces. The helicopter's fuselage inverted. A massive dust cloud was followed by a fireball.

Rigby jumped out of the Land Rover and ran to Kgosi. He found him squatting over Dkari Sibanda's body. The Bushman's face said his thirst for revenge was quenched.

"Did he hurt you?" Rigby asked touching the Bushman's swollen cheek.

"Not too much," Kgosi answered. "He was almost a devil."

Rigby put his hand on Kgosi's shoulder. "Let us tend to our work, my brother."

They set fire to the hook-thorn thicket to protect unsuspecting animals. Kgosi concealed their footprints and the vehicle's tire tracks. The sun was setting now. The unburied dead always wind up in hyenas' bellies. Come morning, they knew the charred helicopter would be the only evidence of what had taken place.

They snuck out of the Chizarira game reserve and headed straight for the border. As they drove, Rigby suggested that Kgosi should consider moving to Victoria Falls. Rigby offered to build him a house and supply the land. He even promised him a job. Now that he was alone, it made sense to move closer to a town. This made no sense to Kgosi. In fact, he found Rigby's offer so ridiculous, he giggled. How could he visit his departed ancestors' graves in the desert? And there was always the possibility of crossing paths with a displaced member of his clan. He thanked Rigby profusely, but he said he was perfectly content living alone in the desert.

Two days later, Rigby dropped Kgosi off at the edge of the

Kalahari. After they said goodbye, Kgosi walked into desert singing to himself. He looked happy to be home. Within minutes, he disappeared into a wavy mirage. Rigby was saddened to see him go, but he smiled nonetheless. The world is a better place with Bushmen in it, he reflected.

28
Six months later

Rigby focused his binoculars on a female white rhino and her calf grazing on a hilltop. Two armed rangers walked slowly behind the rhinos keeping their distance. Rhinos were so endangered they needed to be guarded around the clock. The deaths of Dkari Sibanda and Uncle Mao granted Zimbabwe's endangered animals a reprieve.

The Asian cartel would send a replacement. And it was a safe bet that someone was already moving to take over Sibanda's poaching syndicate. There was just too much money involved. But for now, a peaceful calm settled over the bush veldt.

From time to time, Rigby tried to telephone Lily Rosen, usually after he had been drinking with Otto Bern. He always lost his nerve and hung up before she could answer. As Lily said about a different subject, some stones are better left unturned. He received her postcards, never with a return address and always mailed from an exotic part of the world. These were Lily's temptations. And then suddenly, the cards stopped coming. Somehow, he knew Lily was dead. She had let down her guard and that was the end of it.

He received a letter from Terrance and Jackie Cassidy announcing the birth of their daughter. They had become activists in the wildlife conservation movement.

[249]

Kgosi was reportedly seen a few times on the fringes of the Kalahari. Otto Bern talked about flying to Namibia to search for him, but like so many things in life, the trip was put on the back burner.

High above him two black eagles soared on the afternoon thermals. As Rigby watched them he let the sunshine warm his bronzed face. It felt good to be alive. He was at peace with the world, but he knew the ceasefire was short-lived.

People come and go on the Dark Continent, but Rigby Croxford is as enduring as the land.

JAMES GARDNER

Epilogue
Nelson Mandela:
I dream of an Africa that is in peace with itself.

The Last Rhino is a work of fiction. The extermination of Africa's endangered animals is real. Since 1970, the African rhino population has been reduced by 90%. Today, only 25,000 rhinos survive on the Dark Continent. Last year, 1254 rhinos were killed by poachers in just southern Africa. Rhino horn is coveted by Asians for its make-believe curative properties. The price of rhino horn has risen to $60, 000 dollars per kilogram.

Poachers are killing 30,000 elephants per year. The total population of African elephants is estimated to be 400,000 animals. The ivory is carved into trinkets and figurines. Since 2008, the price of ivory has increased tenfold to $1500 per kilogram. The average African lives on $1 dollar per day. Their dismal reality could mean the extinction of both species in one generation.

What will we tell our grandchildren when these magnificent animals are gone? That we let misguided people kill them and did nothing to stop the carnage? I hope not.

JAMES GARDNER

THE DARK CONTINENT CHRONICLES

THE LION KILLER

DARK CONTINENT CHRONICLES BOOK I

"A riveting thriller...with twists and turns galore."
Robert Halmi, Jr. President & CEO of RHI Entertainment

JAMES GARDNER

"I highly recommend *The Lion Killer*. I have seldom come across such fine descriptive writing in a thriller."

—James Patterson

THE DARK CONTINENT CHRONICLES

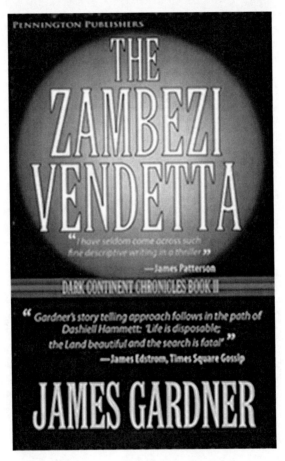

"*A riveting thriller with twists and turns galore.*"

—Robert Halmi Jr.

JAMES GARDNER

THE DARK CONTINENT CHRONICLES

"It's easy to see that Gardner has been there and that he understood what he saw. His powerful writing illuminates the Dark Continent."

—Nelson DeMille

JAMES GARDNER

JAMES GARDNER

James Gardner

JAMES GARDNER

JAMES GARDNER

JAMES GARDNER